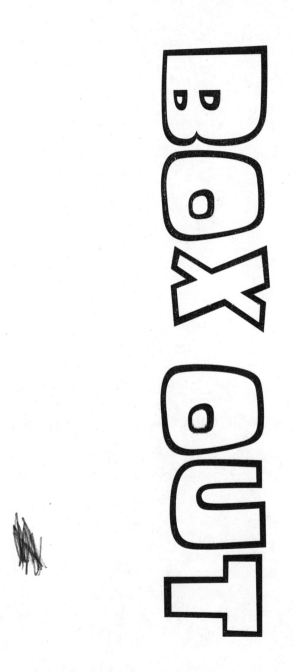

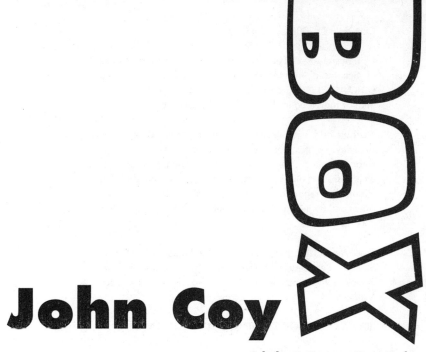

BOX OUT

John Coy

Scholastic Press   New York

LIBRARY OF CONGRESS CATALOGING-IN-PUBLICATION DATA
Coy, John, 1958—
Box out / John Coy.—1st ed.   p.   cm.
Summary: High school sophomore Liam jeopardizes his new position on the varsity basketball team when he decides to take a stand against his coach who is leading prayers before games and enforcing teamwide participation.
ISBN-13: 978-0-439-87032-0
ISBN-10: 0-439-87032-1
[1. Basketball—Fiction.   2. Prayer in the public schools—Fiction.   3. Church and state—Fiction.   4. High schools—Fiction.   5. Schools—Fiction.]   I. Title.
PZ7.C839455Bo 2008   [Fic]—dc22   2007045354

10 9 8 7 6 5 4 3 2 1   08 09 10 11 12

Printed in the United States of America
First edition, June 2008

Text type was set in Futura Book.
Display type was set in Fink Gothic and Futura Extra Bold.
Book design by Marijka Kostiw

FOR MARY, WHO'S GOT GAME

The Call

XXX "Have a seat, Bergie." Coach Kloss points to the metal folding chair in his cramped office. He's a short, solid guy who looks more like a wrestler than a basketball coach.

Liam Bergstrom folds his thin, six-foot-four-inch frame and sits on the edge of the chair. What did he do now?

"Relax," Coach says. "You look like you're expecting to get cut."

Liam exhales a deep breath and his shoulders fall.

"As you've probably heard, Tyler Jensrud broke his leg in two places yesterday. I talked with Coach Grokowsky about who's been playing well on JV. He recommended you and Seth Crowley. You're three inches taller than Seth and I like your upside." He holds one hand higher than the other and gradually raises it above his head. "I'm calling you up, Bergie. You're now on the Horizon High School varsity."

Liam's eyes widen. Varsity — the magic word that's floated in the future. All the running, weights, and practice chasing that goal. Varsity. Did he hear right?

"We're not bringing you up to sit on the bench and look pretty. You're not that pretty." Coach grins and his teeth shine. "Without Jens, we're small up front. We need you to come off the bench and rebound."

"Yes, Coach." Liam's ready to jump out of the chair.

"On varsity, we're family," Coach says. "We're a tight team. If you ever have anything you need to talk about, come on down. My door is open."

"Yes, Coach."

"Be in the locker room by six. We'll have your new uniform ready."

"Thank you, Coach Kloss." Liam reaches his hand out.

"Welcome to varsity, Bergie." Coach shakes it. "We're counting on you."

XXX Liam runs down the hall toward his locker in the old part of the school. He ducks into a classroom to check the time and adds seven hours for France. It's late, but his girlfriend, Mackenzie, should still be up. He spins the combination so fast, he goes past the first number. He tries again, pulls open the locker, and grabs his phone.

"*Allô,*" Mackenzie answers drowsily in French.

"Kenz, Kenz, are you sleeping?"

"No, let me turn on the light. What's going on?"

"I made varsity! Coach just told me! I beat out Seth for the spot!"

"Varsity — that's so awesome." Mackenzie's wide awake now.

"I was shooting for next year." Liam paces in front of his locker. "But it's now. For tonight's game."

"I'm going out with a varsity basketball player. Way cool," Mackenzie says. "I wish I could be there."

"I do, too." She's only been gone two weeks. Sixteen more to go.

XXX "Bow your heads." Coach Kloss kneels on the smooth bench of the boys' locker room.

Liam lowers his head and admires the red number forty-three and the small *H* in a shield above it on his new uniform. This is the first time this jersey has ever been worn. His Nikes tap the double-time beat of pre-game nerves.

Coach closes his eyes. "Lord, help us to play strong. Help

us to do Your work as we take the floor with strong hearts, strong bodies, and strong minds."

Liam folds his hands. Coach G doesn't pray like this on JV. He glances up. Darius Buckner, the sophomore shooting guard who transferred this year from Chicago, stares back at him.

"Let us all join in the prayer You taught us," Coach continues.

"Our Father, who art in heaven, hallowed be Thy name." Liam's voice blends with the others, but Darius is silent. He holds his hands behind his back and looks straight ahead. "And lead us not into temptation, but deliver us from evil." Liam's set to add "amen," but the prayer continues.

"For Thine is the kingdom, and the power, and the glory, for ever and ever. Amen." It's the Protestant version with the extra words that he's not used to.

"Let's get a win." Coach stands.

XXX Liam jogs out of the locker room behind Darius, who has the easy, fluid motion of a basketball star. This is it.

Showtime. Liam stretches to slap the Blazer sign like Darius does as the team runs into the gym.

The pep band blares the school song, and everybody stands and sings. "Go Horizon. Go Horizon. Fight on for our fame. Fight, Blazers, fight, fight, fight. We'll win this game."

Liam's stomach jumps as the sound wraps around the gym. The bleachers are three-quarters full and his mom and dad stand in the parents' section. Mom waves and nudges Dad, who's talking with the friends he plays basketball with.

"We want Liam," Seth shouts. He sits behind the bench with other guys from JV.

Tenths of seconds fly off the clock as Liam wipes his sweaty palms on his warm-up jersey.

"Remember your assignments." Coach squats in front of the starters. "Run the offense, take care of the ball." He looks at Darius, who's adjusting his wristband. "Nothing fancy. On defense, move your feet, deny the passing lanes, and make sure to box out."

The starters stand and everybody presses around Coach as he holds out his open palm. Guys stretch to put their hands on top.

"Horizon High," Coach says.

"Team basketball," everybody shouts.

Liam goes to sit at the end of the bench as the starters walk to the center circle. Everything feels more intense on varsity: Coach's instructions, the crowd's excitement, the senior cheerleaders who swish their tiny skirts in front of the student section across the court. "Hey, hey, it's time to fight! Everybody yell, red and white! Hey, hey, do it again! Everybody yell, go, fight, win!"

Banners line the walls behind the baskets. The girls' basketball team has three state titles and one runner-up. They've won conference six years in a row. Liam does the math. The boys haven't won it in nine years.

"Let's go, Horizon," Mom hollers. Liam rubs the rash on his little finger. She's way too loud.

Jared Drake, the tallest guy on the team, wins the tip, and Darius jets down the floor. He hesitates at the three-point arc, bounces the ball between his legs, then blows by his defender.

An arm hammers his shoulder, but he hangs in the air and makes an acrobatic shot. The Horizon crowd makes a whooshing sound to celebrate the first basket, and kids stomp their feet on the bleachers. Liam stands with his teammates and claps. That was an unbelievable shot. But then that's Darius.

"Run the offense, Buckner," Coach shouts. "Team basketball."

Darius hits the free throw and glides back on defense. He seems so calm, so confident, like he knows what's going to happen on the court before it does. He picks off a pass and flies in for a dunk. Liam jumps up to cheer with everybody else. Darius five, Crosston zero.

XXX With four minutes left in the half, Hunter Nielsen, the bulky center, is a step slow on defense and picks up his second foul. Coach waves for Liam, who rips off his warm-ups. "We're getting killed on the boards, Bergie." Coach puts his hand on Liam's shoulder. "This is why we brought you up. Get out there and grab some rebounds."

Liam wipes his hands on the bottoms of his shoes for a better grip. The horn blares and his heart pounds.

"You got forty-two." Nielsen wipes his cheek. He's got a two-inch scar that runs from his ear to his chin. "Go get 'em."

Liam sizes up his opponent: tall but skinny.

"Who's got shooter?" Drake asks.

"I do." Corey Gund, the point guard, taps his chest. He's short and tough and puckers his lips in a fish face when he's concentrating.

Number thirteen pauses on his release and shoots. Liam pushes back against forty-two to seal him off and grabs the rebound.

"Way to box out, Bergie," Coach shouts.

Gund darts back for the ball and Liam sprints downcourt. He steps out and stands still to set a screen on thirteen to free Gund. Thirteen barges past. These guys are stronger and faster than JV players. Gund shoots a jumper with his lips puckered and Liam rushes to the hoop. He leaps for the rebound but can only get a hand on it, so he taps it to Darius in the corner, who drains a three.

"Way to keep the ball alive, Bergie." Drake claps.

At the other end, Liam chases his man and keeps an eye

out for what's coming. "Left," he hollers to warn Josh Pelke of a screen. Liam pops out to slow the dribbler, then drops back to cover his guy. He stretches out his long arm and picks off a pass.

"Good steal." Gund comes back for the ball and dribbles upcourt. He passes to Darius, who dribbles to the top of the key. Liam steps out to set a screen, but Darius waves him away. He crosses over and rips past his man. Two defenders cut him off, so he bounce-passes to Liam. The ball hits Liam's hands and skips out of bounds.

Liam rubs his palms on his shorts. That was a bullet.

"Run the offense, Buckner." Coach taps his finger to his forehead. "Think out there."

Liam hurries back on defense. Why isn't Coach yelling at him? The pass was right there. He's the one who dropped it.

With twenty seconds left in the half, Horizon is down by nine. Liam cuts to the hoop and is open. Darius zips a pass. Liam glances at his defender, and the ball bounces off his fingers and whaps the Blazer Country mat behind the basket.

Catch the ball. That's the second pass in a row he's missed. "My bad." Liam taps his chest to indicate his fault, but Darius is already running back on defense.

Crosston runs the clock down for the last shot. Forty-two steps out on a screen, and Liam slaps at the ball. It pops free and Darius grabs it and rushes downcourt. Liam chases after as Darius drives in and forces an off-balance shot against two defenders. The ball rolls off the rim as the buzzer sounds.

XXX Terrible. Liam wipes a towel across his face as he sits on the bench in front of his locker. Two turnovers. He's not hanging on to anything. Terrible. What's the matter with his hands? He stares at them as if they'll answer.

Coach walks into the room and looks around. "Down by nine to Crosston. You're playing like individuals, not as a team." He slams a locker. "Bergie, what's the matter with you? Do you have rock hands? Catch the ball."

Liam bites the inside of his cheek. He's got to play better if he wants to stay on varsity.

"Buckner. What are you doing? Run the offense. Run the offense. How many times do I have to tell you? Team basketball," Coach says. "Don't get fancy. Don't try to do too much. Don't act like you're bigger than the team. Run the offense."

Darius looks straight ahead, as if he's in a trance.

"You need to use your head out there." Coach raises his voice. "Basketball requires thinking, not just instinct." He taps his finger to his temple. "Run the offense the way you're supposed to, not one against the world. This is Horizon, not Chicago. We play team basketball here, not street ball."

Darius rises and walks to his locker at the end of the room.

"Come back here." Coach points to the bench.

Darius spins the combination and opens the lock.

"What are you doing?"

Darius pulls the white jersey off his black body and hangs it in his locker. He takes a green, striped shirt off a hanger and puts it on.

"What are you doing?" Coach shouts.

"Quitting," Darius says clearly as he buttons his shirt.

Liam's mouth drops open. He can't do that. He can't walk out in the middle of a game.

"You can't quit on us." Coach shakes his head.

Darius looks calm, as if he knows something that nobody else does. He finishes dressing, puts in his earring, and walks past Coach as if he doesn't exist.

The door clicks and Darius's footsteps echo down the hall. Guys look at one another, but no one says anything. Everybody turns to Coach.

"Bow your heads." His eyes dart around the room. "Let's pray."

Broke

XXX In the second half, Liam scratches his chin as he sits on the bench. *Rock hands.* Why didn't he catch those passes? He won't get back on the floor after playing like that. His first varsity action and he blew it.

Horizon goes on a run and cuts the deficit to two. Liam claps, but he can't stop going over his mistakes. *Rock hands.* If he'd caught those passes, Coach wouldn't have gotten so angry. Darius would still be on the team.

Gund threads a bounce pass to Drake, who knocks down a jumper. The crowd rises and cheers loudly. Tie game.

"That's the way." Coach claps. "We're finally running the offense."

Late in the second half, Nielsen reaches to stop a reverse layup, and the whistle blows. His fourth foul.

Liam checks the clock. Only 3:11 left. Can Nielsen make it to the end without picking up another foul? Forty-two misses the free throw and Pelke grabs the rebound.

On offense, Gund passes to Nielsen on the block. Nielsen

turns and bumps into his defender, who sprawls backward like he's been hit by a truck. The referee blows his whistle and jumps in with his hand behind his head to signal a charge.

Nielsen grimaces. "I hardly touched him."

The ref stares stone-faced as the horn blares to indicate that Nielsen's fouled out.

"Let them play, ref," Mom shouts. Dad tugs at her sweater and encourages her to sit down.

Coach waves for Liam. "Bergie, get in there for Nielsen."

Liam rushes to check in at the scorer's table. *Just let the first half go. Just let the first half go.*

"Let's go, Liam. You can do it." Mom claps.

He pretends not to hear. She can be so embarrassing.

Liam battles through screens to stick with forty-two. He jumps out and waves his arms to cut off the passing angles. The game goes back and forth. Horizon's up by two. Crosston goes up by one, then by three. Chris Staley, the shooting guard who replaced Darius, hits a jump shot, and the Horizon crowd explodes with cheers.

Liam springs for a rebound and passes to Drake, who

misses a jumper. Pelke pressures in the backcourt, and his man bounces the ball out of bounds.

"Time-out. Time-out." Coach jumps up from the bench.

Down by one with thirty seconds left. The subs stand to make room on the bench for the five guys playing so they can sit facing Coach.

"One shot to win." Coach pulls out his whiteboard. "Let's make it a good one."

Liam gulps water like the other guys do, even though he's not thirsty.

"Gund, when the clock's down to ten, look for Drake on the baseline." Coach diagrams it on his board. "Bergie, set a solid screen to free Drake."

Liam nods. *Get good position. Set a solid screen. Hold still.* He puts down the water bottle and wipes his hands on his jersey.

Drake claps. "Let's win this, baby."

The ref blows his whistle and both teams file onto the court. Liam looks at fifty-five, Drake's guy. He's solid, about six-foot-six and built like a linebacker. The ref hands the ball to Pelke, who passes it to Gund. Gund dribbles carefully as the clock ticks down.

Thirteen, twelve, eleven. With ten seconds left, Liam slides into position behind Drake's man. He crosses his arms at the wrist and prepares for contact. Drake cuts past, and fifty-five slams into Liam's shoulder. Drake pops to the baseline and catches the pass. He has a clean look as he rises to shoot. The shot clangs the front rim and bounces off.

Liam leaps and grabs the ball. He's got to shoot fast. He goes up.

Whack. Fifty-five slaps him hard on the elbow and he falls to the floor.

The whistle blows. "Foul on fifty-five, Yellow." The ref jumps in. "Two shots."

"Great play." Drake pulls Liam up from behind.

"You bailed us out." Pelke slaps Liam's hand.

Liam walks to the free throw line. He needs to make one to tie and two to win. He waits for the custodian to finish mopping up his sweat spot from the floor so no one will slip. He positions his feet behind the line and rubs his hands on his shoes. One second left. The game is in his hands. The whole gym quiets, as if silence will make it easier for him.

"Two shots, men." The ref passes the ball to Liam.

Liam bounces the ball and hears the Crosston point guard behind him. "Broke. This shot's broke."

Liam shoots quickly. As soon as he releases, he knows it's short. Way short. He backs off the line, and the ball misses the hoop entirely.

"AIRRRRR BALL! AIRRRRR BALL!" Crosston fans chant.

Liam shakes out his arms. He hasn't shot an air ball from the free throw line in years.

"C'mon, Bergie," Drake says. "You can do it."

Liam approaches the line. *Calm down. Relax. Concentrate.* The cheerleaders cross their fingers and hold on to one another. The ref passes the ball and Liam positions his feet. *Shoot it harder.* He bounces the ball and looks at the hoop.

"Broke," the point guard taunts.

Liam exhales and shoots. Seconds slow and the shot looks good as it arcs toward the hoop.

The ball hits the back of the rim, bounces up, touches the front rim, and rolls off. Forty-two wraps up the rebound as the buzzer sounds. Liam stands at the line and stares at the hoop. All the hundreds — thousands — of free throws he's made. How could he miss both of them? He turns to the scoreboard. Crosston 61, Horizon 60. Game over.

He shuffles to the bench as Crosston fans dance onto the court.

"Get 'em next time." Chris Staley slaps his back.

"Remember this feeling." Coach puts his arm around Liam. "Use it to become a better player. You're on varsity now. We're counting on you."

Liam nods. Coach could have ripped into him and sent him straight back to JV. He could have said he made a mistake and brought Seth up instead.

The rest of the guys head back to the locker room. Nobody else says anything to him. They don't need to. Liam let the team down.

He sees his parents standing at the side of the court. Mom rushes over and gives him a hug. "I'm sorry, Liam."

"Not now, Mom." He frees himself.

"It's okay," Dad says.

"It's not okay." Liam shakes his head. "I lost the game."

"One game, Liam. You have a long season ahead. You'll have other chances."

"Not playing like this." Liam turns and trudges to the locker room.

XXX The January cold slaps Liam's face as he walks to his car after the game. He scrunches his shoulders as he fumbles to insert the key in the lock. It's freezing. Nights like this are when he misses Seattle most. He starts the Toyota and flips the heat to high.

The flat, empty streets of Horizon are quiet. After two and a half years here, he's still getting used to living in a small town. Most of the guys at school have known one another since kindergarten. If you didn't grow up here, you're an outsider.

He turns left at the post office and drives past his church, Saint Mary's, with the statue of Mary holding Jesus in front. Behind the church, lights shine at the one-story, brick nursing home where Grandma lives. Last Sunday they celebrated her eighty-third birthday. Grandma liked the cake and balloons but asked him twice whose birthday it was.

Grandma is the reason they moved here in the first place. After she fell and broke her hip, she couldn't live in her house anymore. Then she had a stroke and started to have memory problems. It was difficult for Dad to keep flying out to see her. So when a job opened up at the elementary school, he applied and they moved. Now Dad visits her every day and bugs Liam to stop by more often.

9:32. Too late to see how she's doing. Besides, what would he talk about? Blowing the game? Missing those free throws was huge. He choked on that first one, but that second shot felt good. That would have tied it and sent the game into overtime. They'd still be playing. They'd still have a chance to win.

Liam drives past the Athletic Building at Borton College, where three guys wearing shorts are carrying basketballs as they walk back to their dorms. Are they crazy? Don't they realize it's freezing?

The team needed Darius on that last possession. He would have made the shot with the game on the line. But he wasn't there because of Liam's stupid turnovers. Liam would give anything to have another chance to catch those passes. His phone breaks the silence.

"That game sucked big time," Seth says in his deep voice.

"Tell me about it." Liam turns the heater down to hear better. "I blew it."

"Don't take it all on," Seth says. "Lots of guys missed shots."

Liam brakes at the four-way stop. "Darius quitting sucks, too."

"What? I thought he got hurt. What happened?"

"I don't know. He walked out while Coach was ripping into him for trying to do too much."

"Well, he was hogging the ball," Seth says. "He didn't pass to anyone."

"He passed to me twice. I dropped it both times. I wouldn't have passed to me after that either."

"Where are you?"

"Right by Connie's Cafe." The car rattles as Liam bumps over railroad tracks.

"We're at Burger King. Come on over."

"Nah. I don't feel like it."

"I'll buy you a Whopper."

"Nah. I want to get home."

"Big baby."

"Later." Liam flips the phone shut as he drives past the turnoff to Mackenzie's house. If she were here, she'd hold him tight and whisper that it's all right. She'd make him feel better. But he can't call her now because it's the middle of the night in France.

He stops at the red light by Lonetree Elementary, Dad's school. No other cars are around and this light takes forever. He could run it. But with his luck tonight, a cop would show and he'd get nailed.

So he replays the dropped passes and missed free throws as he waits and waits and waits for the light to go green.

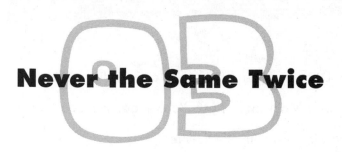

Never the Same Twice

XXX Wednesday morning, Liam finds a parking place in the back lot and turns off the engine. The last thing he wants to do is walk by Jock Corner, where all the senior basketball players hang out. So he pulls down his stocking cap and hikes all the way around the school in the whipping wind.

He hangs his coat in his locker, grabs his books, and shoves them in his backpack. Down the hall, Pelke's locked in a kiss with his girlfriend, Chloe Keenan from the girls' basketball team. Sixteen long weeks until Mackenzie gets back.

"Bergie." Seth's voice rumbles. "Cookieees." Seth rips open a package of Oreos. He's wearing another tight shirt to show off his weight lifting. "Me love cookieees." He has the Cookie Monster voice down.

"Thanks." Liam takes one.

"How you doing?" Seth grabs three.

"Hanging in there." Liam unscrews the top of an Oreo and scrapes the frosting off with his teeth.

"Don't give me that. You're on varsity hoops and going out with Mackenzie Kost. You've got it made." Seth pops Oreos in his mouth like they're candy.

Liam eats the chocolate part of his cookie.

"You got some rebounds last night." Seth holds out the bag.

"You would have, too. I wish we both could have been called up."

"Somebody's got to do the dirty work on JV." Seth bounces back and forth and fakes a punch at Liam's chest. "We won by twelve yesterday."

Liam eats another cookie. "You used up all your fouls?"

"Count on it. A couple of hard fouls get guys thinking."

"I know. I've still got the bruises."

"I helped toughen you up." Seth flexes his biceps in a muscleman pose and other kids turn to look. "If I'd gone against me in practice, I'd have been called up to varsity. Instead I had to go against a wimp."

"Shut up." Liam pushes him. "Next year, we'll play monster defense together."

"Me love defense." Seth holds out the bag again. "Cookieees."

Liam takes two and jams them in his mouth, and he and Seth head in different directions.

Jared Drake comes around the corner and Liam ducks his head.

"Tough break last night." Drake stops and rubs a hand through his short black hair.

"Yeah. I'd like those shots back."

"We should have wrapped it up before then. We should have won by ten."

Liam twists the strap on his backpack. "It's too bad about Darius."

"Who?"

"Darius. Quitting the team."

"Who?"

"Darius Buckner. You know."

"I don't know him." Drake shrugs his shoulders. "I don't know anyone who quits on his teammates."

Liam leans up against a locker and isn't sure what to say.

"Listen, I've got an offer for you." Drake moves closer and Liam smells his aftershave. "Now that you're on varsity, my dad says we can use you for a few hours at the store. Are you interested in a part-time job at Shoe Source?"

"Yeah. I'd love it."

"It's every other Saturday. Not a lot of hours. Seniors get the prime shifts, but you'd still get a forty percent discount on shoes."

"Great." Liam looks down at his worn Nikes. He could use a new pair.

"Noon on Saturday. I'll train you in."

"Thanks." Liam switches his pack to his other arm. "Tell your dad thanks, too."

"Also, remember the meeting tomorrow before school."

"What meeting?"

"HAF."

"What?"

"Horizon Athletic Fellowship," Drake says. "We meet at my house at seven. See you there."

XXX Liam watches the clock during economics, his last class of the day. How can the hands move so slowly? Mr. Einerson diagrams something called elasticity of demand on the board. Twenty more minutes and he can call Kenz. *C'mon, time, move.*

When the period finally ends, he hurries to the industrial tech wing, where the phone reception is better.

Mackenzie picks up after three rings. "Hey, Liam. How was the game?"

"Lousy. I missed two free throws and we lost." He sets his gym bag down on the floor.

"That stinks. Did you lose by a lot?"

"No, one point." He kicks an empty juice bottle down the hall.

"That's t . . . d . . ."

"What?"

"Th . . . te . . . b . . ."

"I can't hear you." Liam moves closer to the window. "You're breaking up."

"Who's breaking up?"

"You were. I couldn't hear you." He stares out at the snow-covered soccer field. He's been waiting all day to call. Now that he's finally talking to her, the words are getting in the way. "How are you doing, Kenz?"

"I'm really homesick. I wish I was back in Horizon. Dad keeps saying what a great opportunity this is to improve my French, but I don't think it's gotten much better. I miss you, Li."

"I miss you more."

"No. Me more. I wish I was snuggled up against you right now."

"I do, too, Kenz."

"I miss so many things: you, my family, the food. Tonight Madame Giroux made coq au vin, but what I'm craving is chicken nuggets. Then she brought out homemade crêpes. She pouts if I refuse, so I had to eat two of them. I've already gained a pound and a half. I'll be a pig by the time I get home. Oink. Oink."

"Stop it." Liam laughs. Even with an extra pound and a half, she's thinner than most girls. "Kenz, I've got to get to practice."

"Ooooh. Your first *varsity* practice?"

"Yeah."

"You'll do great."

"Thanks, Kenz."

"Oink. Oink."

"Stop it. Gotta go." Liam flips the phone closed. Sometimes hearing her voice makes her feel even farther away. He picks up his bag and throws the strap over his shoulder.

On the way to the locker room, he passes girls from the basketball team who are laughing outside the art room.

"Cleared for takeoff." Chloe Keenan runs down the hall and jumps into the arms of Iris Cleary, who twirls her around.

"Hi, Liam." Leah Braverman waves. She's a senior with dark, curly hair and a wide smile.

"Hey." Last year she did an internship with Mom at the Arts Center, and Mom went on and on about how smart and talented she was.

"Let last night go." Her silver nose stud flashes as she turns. "Jack always says the river is never the same twice."

Liam scratches his head. What's that supposed to mean? And who's Jack? "Whatever." Everyone says the girls' team plays silly games and goofs around in practice.

Liam knows Coach Kloss's reputation. His practice isn't going to be anything like that.

Killers

XXX Liam tightens the drawstring on his shorts as he walks down the hall to the small gym behind Gund, Nielsen, and Pelke. He breathes in the new shirt smell of his practice jersey.

"He never fit in." Nielsen pulls his shirt down over his belly.

"He didn't try to," Gund says. "He had an attitude. He wouldn't go to HAF. He wouldn't run the offense. He wanted to do his own thing."

"Admit it." Pelke rolls a ball in his hands. "You were tired of him stealing the ball from you in practice. You're glad he's gone."

"You're the one he dunked on." Gund gives him a shove.

"He always kept to himself." Nielsen adjusts his jock. "Like he thought he was superior."

"What do you expect from someone who hangs around the art room all the time?" Gund says. "Maybe he's gay."

"Gay and a gunner." Pelke bounces the ball off his head soccer style.

"Yeah, he shot the ball every time he got it," Nielsen says.

"The gay gunner," Pelke announces, and the three of them laugh.

Liam follows quietly behind. He should say something. He should stand up for Darius. But these guys are seniors.

"You ready for killers, Big Man?" Pelke tosses the ball to Nielsen.

"Why?"

"Coach is going to be tough after the loss."

Liam's stomach tightens. It wouldn't have been a loss if he'd made his free throws.

XXX "Gather round." Coach Kloss stands at center court. "We've got a lot of work today."

Liam jogs over with the guys. Coach doesn't sound that mad.

"It's simple," Coach says. "We lost last night because we

missed eight free throws in the second half." He holds up eight fingers.

"Bergie, Nielsen, and Drake each missed two. Pelke missed one. So did you, Gund. Eight misses. All we needed was two to win." He adjusts the whistle around his neck. "They're called free throws because they're free points. We've got to have them."

Liam tightens the lace on his left shoe. At least he's not the only one Coach is blaming.

"We were nine of twelve in the first half and five of thirteen in the second. That tells me one thing. What do you think it is?"

"We didn't concentrate enough," Gund says.

"No. Why would we concentrate in the first half and not in the second?"

We choked, Liam thinks, but he's not going to say it. Nobody else says anything either.

"We missed free throws because we were tired. You were bending over with your hands on your knees. That's a sure sign of fatigue. Our conditioning needs to be better, and I take responsibility for that."

Liam stretches his arms behind his back to open up his shoulders. He wasn't too tired last night. He sat on the bench for most of the second half.

"We're supposed to be the best-conditioned team in the conference." Coach raises his index finger. "Number one. Nobody should outwork or outhustle Horizon."

Liam looks down at the floor. This sounds serious.

"Everybody line up for killers." Coach walks to the side.

Everyone hurries to the baseline.

"Go," Coach hollers.

Liam puts his head down and runs with the team. Free throw line, back. Half-court, back. Other free throw line, back. End line and back. Over and over. Running this way feels like punishment.

"Hustle," Coach calls.

It is punishment. Punishment they wouldn't have to suffer if he'd made his free throws.

"Pick up the pace. You're dogging it. I'm going to add extra killers for all of you if one person slacks off."

Liam runs harder and makes sure to touch each line.

"All the way," Coach hollers.

Nielsen, who's the biggest guy, is panting and trailing behind.

"Push yourself." Coach twirls his whistle.

How long will he run them? Maybe until someone drops. Liam isn't going to let it be him. He tries to let his mind go blank to avoid the pain as he runs and runs and runs. When Coach finally blows the whistle, Liam's legs shake like a fawn struggling to stand. He gasps for breath, and his heart beats so fast, it feels like a bomb about to explode.

Nielsen dry heaves at the water fountain, and Liam turns away so Nielsen doesn't see him watching.

"Staley, you're starting shooting guard now." Coach stands under the basket.

Staley, the sandy-haired junior, steps forward.

"First five, we'll run the offense here. Second five, down to that basket." Coach points to the far hoop. "Sharp passes. Solid screens. Show some spirit."

Liam jogs down with the second five and reviews his responsibilities. He lines up and rushes to set a screen on an imaginary opponent.

"That's the way, Bergie." Coach claps.

Liam concentrates on the patterns. It's the same offense he ran on JV, but somehow it feels faster now. As they run it over and over, he makes sure to cut quickly and precisely.

Coach Kloss blows his whistle. "Everybody down here. Two-on-two rebounding drill. Crosston had eleven more rebounds last night. We need to do a better job of boxing out."

He motions Drake forward. "If I'm on defense guarding Drake, I need to stay close to him. As soon as the shot goes up, I box out by pushing back with my butt and hips to keep him away from the hoop." Coach squats down and pushes Drake past the free throw line. "That way I can grab the rebound."

Coach looks around at the guys. "You can't rebound if you don't box out. Some of you are not showing enough energy." He looks around the group. "First four, out here. Box out."

Nielsen slams back and catches Liam off balance. Liam struggles to hold his ground, but Nielsen stays with him and drives him out. Liam can't be so passive against somebody so bulky. He has to use his quickness.

"Switch," Coach calls.

Liam pushes against Nielsen and keeps his body on him as they battle for inside position. Coach shoots from the free throw line and the ball bounces up. Liam holds off Nielsen and grabs the ball.

"That's it, Bergie. Box out and protect your space. Nielsen, you're playing too soft. You need to want it more." Coach hits his fist against his palm. "Switch."

Nielsen takes the inside position and this time Liam pivots quickly to the baseline. He slides past, rushes to the hoop, and reaches up to snag the ball as it comes off the other side.

"Too slow, Nielsen," Coach says. "Show some hustle."

Guys switch partners and Liam goes up against Drake and then Pelke. He pushes and shoves and bounces around like a pinball, going hard after every shot.

"Way to fight, Bergie," Coach calls. "We brought you up to rebound. We've got plenty of guys who want to shoot on this team. What we need are some rebounders."

Nielsen pushes Liam in the back and stretches for a long rebound. He pulls the ball in and swings his elbows, cracking Liam in the jaw.

Liam bends over and checks to make sure his teeth are still in place.

"You okay, Bergie?" Staley asks.

"Yeah." Liam looks at Nielsen, who's lining up for the next rebound. Was that an accident? Or was it payback for showing up a senior?

After everybody is exhausted, Coach blows his whistle and motions for the team to gather under the basket. "We're eight and six now. We need a win at Plainview." He twirls his whistle. "Each of you has a role on this team. If you concentrate on your role, we'll succeed." He catches the whistle. "Team basketball. We need to run our offense. Nothing fancy. Nothing clever. Don't try to do too much."

Liam pulls at his sweaty T-shirt. That's what Coach told Darius last game. He hasn't said anything about him. Just like Drake, he's acting as if Darius were never part of the team.

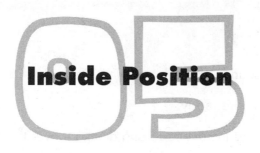

Inside Position

X X X "What's for dinner?" Liam shrugs off his coat and grabs a hanger.

"Chicken enchiladas, black beans, rice, and salad." Dad turns down *All Things Considered* on the kitchen radio. Dizzy, their black cat, meows around in a circle, and Liam bends down to pet her quickly.

"I'm starving." He washes his hands with a squirt of Dawn at the sink.

"Here." Dad slides him an avocado. "Cut this for the salad. Your mom should be here any minute." He passes a cutting board over. "How was practice?"

"Coach was upset about the missed free throws. Everybody's, not just mine." Liam stands at the counter next to Dad. Dad's still taller, but not by much.

"What else did he say?"

"That we need to be the best-conditioned team in the conference." Liam picks a pecan from the salad and pops it in his mouth.

"That sounds like a lot of fun." Dad clicks on the oven light. "These are ready."

Liam slices the avocado and dumps it over the lettuce.

"What smells so good?" Mom rushes in, sets down her leather case, and sheds her long coat. She brushes her black hair back and her bracelets clink.

"Enchiladas." Liam turns his cheek for Mom's kiss. Her breath smells like garlic. "Did you eat at Martelli's again for lunch?"

"Yes, why?"

"Nothing."

"Hi, honey." She and Dad lock lips like they've been apart for a week. Then she opens the drawer next to the dishwasher. Dizzy recognizes the sound and races to the rug by the back door, where Mom kneels down with the blue-handled brush.

"That's a baby," Mom coos as she brushes her with long strokes. Dizzy rolls around on her back in ecstasy. "How was school, Liam?"

"Okay. Coach said the whole team was responsible for the loss."

"That's true."

"But he didn't mention Darius at all. That was weird."

"What?"

"He acted like Darius was never on the team." Liam pours dressing on the salad.

"Wasn't Darius the best player?" Mom looks up from brushing Dizzy.

"Yeah, but Coach and some of the seniors didn't like his game." Liam grabs two salad spoons from the jar and sticks them in the bowl. "Coach emphasizes team basketball, and Darius plays too much one-on-one. At last night's game, Coach criticized him for playing street ball and not using his head."

"Does he say things like that to any of the white players?" Mom stands up and washes her hands.

"No."

"That school has a problem it's not facing up to. Some of those teachers act like they have a homogeneous group of white kids when they don't anymore. They need to join the twenty-first century."

"Slow down, Kate," Dad says. "Horizon's changing."

"At the speed of a glacier." She rips off a paper towel.

"New people are moving in and attitudes are shifting."

"Yeah, but people here are so hesitant to challenge the way things have always been done."

"Dinner's served." Dad carries the steaming pan of enchiladas to the table. "Let's pray."

Liam reaches out to his parents: Mom with her cold hand and jangly bracelets and Dad with his big hand that's warm from the enchiladas.

"*Mmmm,* smells delicious." Mom watches Dad scoop up an enchilada for her. "What else is new at school, Liam?"

"Nothing." He does fine in school — As and Bs — but Mom's always on him to do better.

"Have you been studying vocabulary for the PSAT?" She reaches for her napkin.

"Yeah." He passes his plate to Dad.

"What chapter are you up to?"

"I've got tons of time. I don't take it until next year."

"Don't procrastinate." Mom smooths the napkin in her lap. "The PSAT determines National Merit scholarships and it's good preparation for the SAT. Those scores determine your college choices, so you need to give yourself the best opportunity."

Liam chews his enchilada. She's so extreme. She obsesses so much about the PSAT, you'd think *she* was taking it.

XXX "Let that last game go." Seth pours hot sauce on his taco the next day at lunch. "Forget about it."

Liam pushes lettuce around on his plate and tries to shut out the din echoing off the cafeteria walls.

"Quiet down," Mr. Einerson, the lunchroom monitor, hollers.

"We beat Plainview by thirty on JV." Seth sniffs his sugar cookie and takes a bite.

"But this is varsity."

"They're terrible on varsity, too," Seth says. "Plainview's always good in wrestling and terrible at hoops."

"I hope that's true tonight."

"Count on it. They're so bad, they'll make anyone look good."

Liam crunches his taco. "Thanks . . . I think."

At the next table, three cute girls with straight hair and lots of eye shadow whisper.

Liam looks over and they giggle. "Friends of yours?" He turns to Seth.

"They're ninth-grade cheerleaders," Seth says. "They're into you, not me. You're the big varsity player."

XXX In the first half of the game, Liam sits on the bench, tapping his heel. The whistle blows and Nielsen picks up another cheap foul.

"Move your feet. Don't reach with your arms. How many times do I have to tell you?" Coach pleads. "Bergie, go in for Nielsen."

Liam peels off his warm-ups and rushes to the scorer's table.

"Box out and grab some rebounds," Coach says.

Liam sets a screen and Staley hits a wide-open shot.

"Nice work." Staley slaps his hand.

Plainview turns it over on a traveling call, their third in three trips down the floor. Seth is right. They're terrible. It's easy to see why they haven't won a conference game this year. Gund shoots from the top of the key with his lips puckered and the ball bounces off the rim. Liam grabs it and goes back up for two.

"Good board," Gund calls.

On defense, Liam boxes out his guy to keep him away from the hoop. He watches the shot and anticipates where the miss will bounce off. On offense, he fights for openings and pushes past his guy to grab the ball. So much of rebounding is desire, about wanting the ball more than anybody else.

Drake fumbles a pass in the post and Liam dives for the loose ball. Hands reach to take it away from him. "Time-out. Time-out," he calls.

The ref blows his whistle. "Time-out, Red."

"That's the way to fight for the ball." Coach pats Liam on the back. "That's the type of hustle we need."

Liam sits with the starters as Coach diagrams the out-of-bounds play on his whiteboard. "Time for one shot. Drake, set a back screen for Staley. Staley, break to the corner. Bergie, hit Staley with the pass when he comes off the screen."

Staley turns to Liam. "After you pass it, go straight

to the hoop. You can beat your guy for inside position if I miss."

"Okay." Liam nods. He feels more a part of the team than he did last game.

"Red ball." The ref points to the spot. Liam takes the ball and waits for his teammates to set up in their four corner positions. He slaps the ball to start the play and Nielsen sets the screen. Staley flies to the corner. Liam delivers the pass and then rushes to the hoop for the rebound. Staley buries it.

"That's the way," Coach shouts. "Team basketball."

As the first-half buzzer sounds, Drake approaches Liam. "Good hustle."

"Thanks." Liam wipes sweat off his face with his jersey.

"We missed you this morning."

"What?" Liam panics. Was there an early practice?

"HAF," Drake says as they walk to the locker room. "I told you about it."

"Sorry. I forgot."

"Don't forget. Every Thursday morning at my house. I expect you to be there."

XXX In his room, Liam picks up the framed picture of Mackenzie from his desk. Her dark hair hangs down to her shoulders and her mouth is half open in a sexy smile. He looks into her brown eyes and imagines kissing her good night.

A raw-red floor burn stings his left knee. He must have picked it up diving for the ball. He didn't feel it during the action, but now it hurts. It's a small price to pay for such a good game.

He burrows under his duvet as the wind whips against the window. "Hail Mary, full of grace," he recites the words Mom taught him as a kid. He's said them so many times that their rhythm is comforting. He's grateful to Coach for giving him so many minutes. He's grateful that he played well. He's grateful that they won by twenty-two and nobody got hurt.

He thinks about his day and how he treated people and what he could have done better. He didn't get into any major arguments with anyone. Mom was sleeping by the time he got back, so he didn't argue with her about cleaning up his room, preparing for his future, or wiping up cat vomit.

He rolls over onto his back. He could have gotten up early this morning and gone to see Grandma. She might have liked that. There's lots more stuff like that he could do to be a better person.

He prays a final Hail Mary and gives thanks for his first varsity win, even though Plainview stinks.

XXX "Did you get my package yet?" Mackenzie asks the second Liam answers his phone.

"No. What is it?"

"A secret. I can't tell."

"Give me a clue." Liam tosses clothes around as he looks for the uniform Drake gave him to wear to work today.

"It's something French."

"Big surprise. Let me guess. A black beret."

"No, nothing to wear. No more questions. I don't want to give it away."

"French bread, French fries, a French kiss."

"Stop it," she says. "Though I'd like to give you the last one. I've got to go in a couple of minutes. Someone's picking me up."

"Where are you going?"

"A dance. Here in Arles."

"Who are you going with?"

"Some friends from school."

"Which friends?" Liam stares out the window at the bare branches.

"Jacqueline and Phillippe. Bernadette and Georges. Jean-Baptiste."

Liam goes quiet. Sounds like couples going to a dance.

"What's up there?" Mackenzie asks eagerly.

"Not much." Dizzy jumps up on the bed, but Liam pushes her off.

"Did you have a game Thursday?"

"We beat Plainview." Liam sits down on the rumpled sheets.

"How'd you do?"

"Two points. Six rebounds."

"That's good."

"I miss you, Kenz." He hears someone talking French in the background.

"I miss you, too, Li. I've got to go. My ride's here."

"Who's giving you a ride?"

"Just a friend. Jean-Baptiste. Gotta go."

Liam snaps shut the phone that's already dead.

Jean-Baptiste is probably handsome, rich, and drives a Ferrari. What's Mackenzie doing going to a dance with him? He tosses the phone on the chair. He's not going anyplace with other girls. He and Mackenzie didn't talk about it exactly, but he thought they had an understanding.

Jean-Baptiste. What a stupid name.

XXX Later that afternoon, Liam straightens display models at Shoe Source at the Prairieview Mall. So many cool shoes to use his discount on. Drake's already shown him how to use the register, process credit cards, and remove the security tags. Liam examines his black pants, black Nikes, and black-and-white referee's shirt in the mirror. He pulls at the shirt. He looks dorky dressed up like a referee, but Drake insists it sells shoes.

The entrance bell rings. "Your turn, Bergie." Drake nods at a short woman with huge sunglasses.

"Can I help you?" Liam's zebra shirt reflects back at him.

"Yes, I need new shoes for my Pilates class." The woman makes it sound urgent.

"I didn't think you wore shoes in Pilates."

"No, not *in* class. I need the right shoes to wear *to* class." She fluffs up the back of her hair.

"Over this way." Liam leads her to the walking shoes. "Any of these would work to go to class."

"Thanks. I'll look around." The woman lifts her glasses to study a pair of Pumas.

"Let me know if you want to try anything on."

Liam and Drake watch ESPN Classic on the TV above the desk. Dennis Rodman battles through two defenders to grab an offensive rebound for the Chicago Bulls. "What's the deal with Rodman's hair?" Drake makes a face like he's swallowed a toad.

"I think he dyed it team colors for the playoffs."

"Red and black? Together? Weird."

Michael Jordan misses and Rodman grabs another board. "Yeah, but he sure can rebound." Rodman sets a screen and charges to the hoop when Scottie Pippen's bank shot rolls off. Rodman tips the rebound to himself, and the Chicago crowd goes nuts. He's a rebounding machine. Jordan delivers a no-look pass to Pippen, who finishes with a left-handed jam, and Rodman pumps his fist to the fans.

The sunglasses woman waves as she leaves the store. "Nothing had the right energy. Thanks anyway."

"Thanks for stopping." Liam turns back to the game. Can't beat getting paid to watch old basketball games.

"Check this out." Drake gives Liam a red band with the letters HWJC on it.

"What is it?"

"My dad got a bunch of them," Drake says. "HWJC stands for How Would Jesus Compete? You wear it in games as a reminder. Try it on."

Liam stretches the band over his wrist. How would Jesus compete? He tries to imagine Jesus on the court for Horizon. More likely Jesus would be in drama, maybe have a small part in *Man of La Mancha,* the winter play. Or band. Yeah, Jesus would play saxophone in the band.

"So we'll see you at HAF this week." Drake puts his red band on.

"Yeah. I'll be there." Liam runs his fingers over the letters. Why does Drake keep bugging him about this?

"Good, we need you. HAF builds team spirit, and Coach wants boys' hoops to set an example for other sports. He wants everybody on the team to be there."

XXX "He who exalts himself will be humbled, he who humbles himself will be exalted." Father Connell's deep voice booms as he paces back and forth in front of the congregation.

Father Connell is short and rumpled and taught Liam's confirmation class. Liam likes that he doesn't take himself too seriously.

"Humility is not merely a virtue," Father Connell says. "Humility is a necessity for a person of faith."

Liam pulls his coat around his shoulders and notices Coach G in the third row with his wife and daughter. It's freezing in here. The heat must go straight up to the ceiling. He keeps thinking about Mackenzie. He remembers when he made JV and finally got up the guts to ask her out. He couldn't believe it when she said yes. He can still picture the pink sweater she wore on their first date and how good she looked in it. The guys on JV were jealous that he was going out with her. Even the varsity guys started to notice his existence.

That was two months ago. She's going to be in France for much longer than that. What did she do last night at the dance? Where did she go afterward? What else did she do with Jean-Baptiste?

"All rise," Father Connell says.

Liam stands. He can't get the image of Mackenzie with some rich, handsome French guy out of his mind.

XXX "Hey, Darius. What's that?"

"What?" Darius is coming out of the art room carrying a brown, two-foot-tall, triangular tower as kids pour into the hall.

"What you're holding," Liam says.

"Ceramic sculpture." The angular head of a person is etched into one side.

"Cool." Liam keeps looking at the distinctive face. The expression on it is almost a mixture of strength and fear. "Hey, sorry about those dropped passes against Crosston."

"Forget it." Darius turns and walks down the hall.

"No, they were right there. I should have had them." Liam follows him.

"That's true."

"If I'd caught them, Coach wouldn't have gone off on you, and you'd still be on the team." Liam fingers the strap of his backpack.

"Listen, you did me a favor." Darius doesn't break his stride. "I can't play for Kloss. He disrespected me with that talk about street ball. He doesn't know hoops. He doesn't respect the game."

"Still, I can't believe you quit. You're good enough to earn a scholarship."

"My dad's been on me to quit for a month." Darius turns the corner and Liam hurries to keep up. "He says if I put half the energy into art that I put into hoops, I'll have plenty of scholarships."

"So you quit because of your dad?" Liam asks.

"No. I quit because I hate Kloss. That's enough."

"I know, but you didn't like the prayers either, did you?"

"They didn't bother me."

"But you didn't say them."

"What are you? A cop? I get ready for games my own way."

"Sorry." Liam tries to think of something else to talk about. "We won by twenty-two at Plainview."

"Look at me." Darius turns to Liam. "Do I look like I care?"

Liam tightens the strap on his pack and shakes his head. Maybe the guys are right. Maybe Darius doesn't care about anybody other than himself.

No Turnovers

XXX When Liam gets home, he finds a package addressed to him on the kitchen counter.

"Who's it from?" Mom looks up from her laptop.

"Mackenzie."

"Oh."

Liam rips off the paper. Mom's never been nuts about Mackenzie. She doesn't think Mackenzie's good enough or smart enough for her boy. Too bad. Mackenzie's his girlfriend, not hers.

Inside is a cardboard box covered with tape. It looks like the box was sealed to survive a hurricane. He slices through the tape with scissors.

"Be careful." Mom looks up but continues to type.

Liam cuts through the last section and pulls out a purple box labeled CHOCOLATERIE MONIQUE.

"Oh, my." Mom gets up. "French chocolate."

Liam peels the wrapping off the box slowly while Mom

watches. She's practically drooling. He opens the box and takes a sniff. *"Mmmm."*

"Are you going to share?"

"Are you going to say something nice about Mackenzie?"

"Yes." Mom looks closely at the chocolates. "She picks out wonderful gifts."

"More." Liam holds the box in front of her and she follows him around the living room.

"She's a thoughtful girl."

"More."

"She's a lovely young woman."

Liam laughs. "See, that wasn't so bad. Have a chocolate."

Mom picks one, smells it, and takes a bite. "Delicious."

Liam selects a chocolate-covered hazelnut. Mackenzie must be missing him. Or maybe she's feeling guilty about something.

XXX Liam pulls the laces of his Nikes tight and twists them into a double knot before the game on Tuesday.

West Branch is Horizon's main rival, so these games are always intense. The gym will be packed tonight.

"Take care of the basketball." Coach waves his arms like an umpire signaling safe. "These guys are twelve and two. If we want to beat them, we can't turn the ball over." He's wearing a red HWJC band and a sweater vest that says HORIZON BASKETBALL.

How much would someone have to pay Liam to wear a vest like that? A lot. Enough for a plane ticket to France.

"Staley, will you lead us in prayer?" Coach kneels on the bench.

Staley steps forward and Liam folds his hands. Does everybody on varsity have to do this? Is he going to have to lead prayers, too?

"Lord, we ask You to guide us," Staley says. "Be with us tonight as we compete the right way. Protect us as we do Your work."

Liam looks around. All the other guys are wearing their HWJC bands. He didn't think it was mandatory. His own wrist looks naked in comparison.

"Let us pray together," Staley says.

"Our Father, who art in heaven, hallowed be Thy name." Liam bows his head and waits for the Protestant ending.

"For Thine is the kingdom, and the power, and the glory, for ever and ever. AMEN." Everybody hits the last two syllables with extra volume.

"Let's go get a victory." Coach stands.

Liam slaps the Blazer sign as he runs into the gym. The bleachers are full and the crowd cheers loudly. He spots his folks in the same seats as last time. Mr. Craney, the high school principal, is talking to someone who's painted his chest and face red and white. It's Seth.

"Beat the crap out of them," Seth hollers.

Craney glares at him.

"Snot," he says. "Knock the snot out of them."

West Branch comes onto the floor and their fans roar. It sounds like they have as many people here as Horizon does — not much of a home-court advantage. The West Branch players form a circle and pass two balls back and forth. They've got some big guys, and they're smiling and cracking jokes. They look confident, like they can't imagine losing to Horizon.

XXX On the opening tip, West Branch controls the ball, and Horizon rushes back on defense.

"Hands up," Coach calls.

West Branch sends the ball into the post and back to the arc. Staley rushes out, but Collinswood, West Branch's all-state guard, rises over him and buries the jumper.

"Get on him," Coach shouts.

On offense, Horizon doesn't get any open looks because of suffocating man-to-man defense.

"Keep moving," Coach hollers.

Staley cuts off Pelke's screen, but Collinswood sticks to him. Gund passes to Nielsen, who looks like he's not sure what to do. Nielsen throws a high pass to Drake and the West Branch center picks it off easily.

"No turnovers." Coach looks down the bench. "Bergie, get in for Nielsen. Take care of the ball."

Collinswood drives to the hoop and draws a foul on

Nielsen. Liam rips off his warm-ups, checks in, and runs onto the court.

"Bergie, Bergie," Seth bellows, and some of the guys from JV join in. "Bergie, Bergie."

"You've got forty-five." Nielsen breathes hard.

Liam lines up for the free throw and wipes his hands on the soles of his shoes.

"Two shots." The ref bounces the ball to Collinswood.

Liam looks over at forty-five. He's about the same height, but maybe twenty pounds heavier. Liam's going to have to stay in front of him to keep him off the boards.

Collinswood nails the free throw and steps back from the line. He makes the game look so easy. He spins the ball and knocks down the second one.

Liam grabs the ball and starts to pass it, but at the last second he sees Collinswood pressing. He pulls back and signals for time.

The ref blows his whistle. "Time-out, White."

"Smart call, Bergie." Staley jogs with Liam to the bench.

"Drake, you need to help out on the press. Pay

attention." Coach pulls out his whiteboard. "Nielsen, get in for Drake."

Drake spits out his mouth guard and walks to the end of the bench. Coach is pulling guys as soon as they make a mistake. It's hard to get into the flow of the game that way.

"Nielsen, come back on the press." Coach diagrams Xs and Os on the board. "Bergie, get the ball to Nielsen."

Liam nods.

"Run the offense." Coach sets the whiteboard down and holds out his palm. "Horizon High."

"Team basketball," everybody shouts.

Liam walks onto the court prepared for the press, but West Branch takes it off and switches to a one-three-one zone. They're not predictable. They keep switching looks and keeping Horizon off balance.

He runs the offense and West Branch anticipates it. Forty-five grabs Liam's shirt but keeps his hands in so he doesn't get caught. Pelke shuffles a soft pass and Liam jumps for the layup.

Whaap. Someone knocks the ball out of bounds. The West Branch fans go wild, but the ref blows his whistle.

"Foul on number twenty-one, Green. Two shots."

Collinswood looks at the ref. "All ball." He smiles as he walks past.

Liam rubs his palms. Collinswood is right. The block was clean. Where did he come from? He seemed to swoop out of the sky.

"Don't you know a block when you see one?" a West Branch fan howls in protest.

"Open your eyes, you blind bat." A heavy guy in a green sweater takes off his glasses and waves them at the ref. "That's no foul."

Liam steps to the line for free throws he doesn't deserve. The ref passes him the ball. Free points, Coach called them. Nobody guarding you. Nobody waving a hand in your face. Free points. Yeah, but Coach isn't the one trying to knock them down with all these people screaming.

Broke. The word from the Crosston game echoes in his mind. The first shot bounces off the side of the rim.

"One shot, fellas." The ref gives Liam the ball.

Liam bounces it twice, looks up, and shoots. It hits the

front of the rim, pops up, and drops in. One of two. Why can't he relax and make two of two like he did on JV?

Back on defense, Liam gets up on his toes and moves to cut off the passing lane. As the ball moves around, he switches between playing in front of his guy to playing behind, so West Branch can't pass it in easily. He boxes out his guy and jumps for a rebound.

"That's our Bergie," Seth's voice rumbles.

Late in the half, Gund signals for the last shot. As many mistakes as they've made, Horizon is only down by eleven. A hoop here would cut it to single digits. Gund bounces the ball at the top of the key as the clock counts down.

Liam sets a screen on Pelke's man. Gund passes to Pelke, who passes back to Staley. Collinswood is all over him. Staley passes to Liam, whose guy guards him tightly. He feeds Nielsen, who hesitates and passes back to Gund.

Gund shoots a jumper as the buzzer sounds. Rejected. What a bad shot. Everybody was playing cautiously, trying to avoid a turnover rather than making a move to the basket.

What did Darius call it? Not respecting the game.

Greater Glory

XXX After the game, Liam sits silently in front of his locker. Another loss. Sixty-four to fifty, and West Branch played its second string the final ten minutes. He got a lot of time, though, because Drake and Nielsen kept making mistakes and getting pulled. Three points and seven rebounds — a solid game. Collinswood even told him "good work" when they slapped hands.

Liam unties his shoes. West Branch plays a fun style of ball. They know they're good and they've got the record to prove it, but it's more than that. Their coach lets them play. He doesn't pull them the minute they make a mistake. On defense, they gamble for steals. On offense, they take the ball to the hoop expecting to score. They usually do.

He pulls off his left shoe and notices dried blood on his sock. He gently feels the toe. Somebody must have stepped on his foot. He'll deal with it when he gets home. He gets dressed and heads out into the cold. Snow is falling so hard, he can't see the end of the parking lot.

The Toyota whirrs in protest and then fires up. He turns on the wipers and rolls the windows down and up to clear them off. He flips on the defroster for the back. That beats getting out and brushing snow in the cold.

The radio blasts as he drives. He focuses on the white line on the side as snow dances down in the dark. Right before J & S Auto, something's on the pavement. He slows to avoid a deer that's been hit. Its legs point in different directions and guts color the snow. He drops his speed and concentrates on the road.

If only Mackenzie were here to make him feel better. What's she doing now? Sleeping. But what did she do today? Was she with that Jean-Baptiste guy again?

Liam pulls off the paved road onto the gravel one and then into the driveway. On nights like this, it would be nice to have a bigger garage so he could park in it, too. Snowflakes flicker against the dark sky, and he sticks out his tongue and catches one.

Inside, Dad's sitting on the floor, listening to Wynton Marsalis as he cuts construction paper in the shape of beetles for his kindergartners. Mom's reading *Newsweek* on the couch with Dizzy curled up in her lap.

"You played well." Dad stops cutting.

"Thanks."

"West Branch is impressive. Collinswood controls the game at both ends of the floor."

Liam remembers the block. "Yeah, he's good."

"We ate earlier," Mom says. "There's lasagna left. And apple pie."

"I'll shower first."

Liam checks his e-mail. Plenty of spam: stock tips, security alerts, and the all-time, best ever, money back guarantee for increasing sperm quantity. But nothing from Mackenzie.

He pulls off his bloody sock. The nail on his fourth toe has cut into the skin of the middle one. He turns the shower to hot and gets in. The water pounds his back. He doesn't move as his muscles soak up the heat, and he's transported past thought to basic physical sensation: sore, hungry, exhausted. His bloody toe stings as soap washes over it.

He's in the shower so long, the room steams up and the

moist air loosens his lungs. He hacks up a greenie and spits it in the toilet. When he's finished, he dries himself with a fluffy towel, clips the toenail, and wraps a Band-Aid on it. Now he's starving.

XXX Mom gives him a glass of water and presses the reheat button on the microwave. "How do you feel?"

"Okay."

"How come Coach Kloss is so critical?" She sits down across the counter from him.

"What do you mean?" Liam takes a long drink.

"The West Branch coach encourages his players calmly and explains things. He acts like a teacher. Coach Kloss shouts and gets angry."

"He doesn't like to lose. None of us do." Liam finishes his glass of water. One of the drawbacks of being an only child is there's no one else for Mom to cross-examine.

"Coach G wasn't like that."

"Mom, that was JV."

"So?" The microwave dings and she gets the plate of lasagna and corn.

"Varsity's different, Kate." Dad punches a hole in a beetle book and attaches a fastener. "Coach Kloss does a good job. He's been coaching this way for a long time."

Liam dives into his lasagna.

Mom picks up her magazine. "That doesn't mean he can't change."

XXX At his locker, Liam flips through his notebook, looking for his English homework. He's sure he did it. Where is it?

"Hi, Liam." Leah is half hidden behind a huge canvas. Darius holds the other end and Iris Cleary carries their backpacks.

"Hey."

"Too bad about West Branch," she says. "Collinswood is tough, isn't he?"

"Yeah. Do you know him?"

"I played with him in the summer. He's a good guy."

"How'd you do last night?"

"We won by twenty-six. Iris dominated inside when Jessica twisted her ankle."

Liam turns to Iris. She's tall and pretty with blue eyes and short blond hair. "Way to go."

"Thanks." She smiles shyly.

"Do you mind?" Darius says. "I don't want to hold this all day."

"Sorry." Liam walks to the other side. "What is it?"

"A new painting of Leah's," Iris says. "I helped her with it, and we're going to hang it in the library."

Swirls of purple and blue blend on a background of black. "I like it. What's it called?"

"*Missing Shea,*" Iris says as she follows Leah and Darius. The painting moves down the hall like a sailboat cutting across a lake.

Liam watches Iris's blond hair in the crowd. She's tall, taller than Darius. He wishes he didn't have English. Hanging a painting with them sounds like more fun than being bored by Mrs. Stabenow.

XXX Thursday morning, Liam rubs his freshly shaved cheek as he drives down Drake's street. He promised he'd be here, but at this hour he'd much rather be back in bed.

Cars line both sides of the street, but Liam finds a spot behind Pelke's Durango. He and Pelke slam their doors at the same time.

"Do you always come to these HAF meetings?" Liam jams his keys in his pocket.

"Yeah. It's really important to Coach Kloss."

"So is it kind of like church or something?" Liam gets a whiff of Pelke's strong cologne.

"I don't know," Pelke says. "I don't go to church. I'm here because I want to keep starting."

Liam kicks a chunk of ice off his wheel well. "That's pretty cynical."

"No, it's not. It's smart. It's insurance."

Seth's Silverado speeds around the corner. Seth skids on some ice, straightens it out, and crunches into a spot down the street.

"I'll wait for him," Liam says.

"See you inside." Pelke hurries toward the big house.

"Bergie." Seth bounds out of his truck.

"I didn't know you'd be here." Liam dances from one foot to another trying to stay warm.

"Drake invited me." Seth's wearing his letter jacket unzipped.

Liam's breath forms small clouds. "Let's get inside. I'm freezing."

XXX "You finally made it." Drake greets them in the entryway. He extends his hand and Liam shakes it.

Liam unzips his coat and glances at the sparkling chandelier above their heads. He hears the hum of voices and girls giggling in the kitchen.

"Coats down there." Drake wears a tan shirt that says GREATER GLORY on the pocket. "Food in the dining room."

Liam follows Seth downstairs to a huge room dominated by a TV the size of a movie screen.

"Wow," Seth whispers. "I didn't realize there was so much money in shoes."

Liam drops his coat onto the long leather couch. DVD cases line the wall behind it. "There must be a million movies here." He scans the titles.

Seth pulls on the sleeves of his long-sleeve T-shirt. "Let's see what they have to eat."

The kitchen and dining room are crowded, so Liam follows Seth, who bulldozes a path to the table. Breads, muffins, and bagels sit on silver trays.

"Is Drake on some kind of health kick?" Seth makes a face like he's sick. "I need a doughnut."

Liam chooses a cinnamon-raisin bagel and smothers it with honey-walnut cream cheese. He watches Pelke pour a glass of grapefruit juice for his girlfriend, Chloe. For someone who's only here because he has to be, Pelke seems to be having a good time.

Liam slides over to get juice and sees Coach Kloss coming toward him.

"Bergie, I'm glad you made it." Coach slaps him on the back. "One hundred percent — everyone from varsity basketball is here."

Staley and a senior with red hair stand in front of the fireplace and motion for quiet. "I'm Chris Staley from basketball."

"And I'm Trisha Norwood from swimming. For anybody new, we're your HAF co-captains."

"Thanks for being here," Staley says. "This is our largest turnout of the year."

Everybody claps and Coach beams.

"For the warm-up, we want you to break up into small groups of four or five and introduce yourself." Trisha twirls a strand of hair around her finger. "Tell the group which sport you play and share a triumph and a challenge. A triumph is something good that's happened and a challenge is something you're struggling with."

Circles form on the living room carpet and Liam and Seth join the nearest one. Trisha gestures to Liam. "Why don't you begin?"

"I'm Liam Bergstrom and I play basketball." Liam tries to think of a triumph. "I've been on varsity for a little over a week and I'm doing pretty good." He hopes it doesn't sound like bragging, especially in front of Seth.

"And a challenge?" Trisha encourages him with a smile.

Liam taps his heel. "My girlfriend is in France for four

months. That's a gigantic challenge." He turns to the left to indicate he's finished.

"My name's Chloe Keenan. I play basketball and my triumph is finding people in my life I can really count on." She smiles at Pelke. "My challenge was having to work with Jared Drake to set up the food for this meeting."

Liam laughs with the others and Chloe grins. Her brown hair is pulled back in an orange headband. She's pretty in a perky sort of way.

"My real challenge is my younger sister," she says. "I'm worried about the friends she's hanging out with." Liam watches others nod sympathetically. Chloe's challenge is caring about someone else. Maybe that's what he was supposed to say. He should have said something about Grandma.

After everybody finishes, Staley introduces Drake. "As you know, some of us have been working on our own Champion's Prayer." Drake gives copies to Chloe, who passes them around the room. Drake waits until everybody has one. "Let's all read the first two verses together."

"'God, You are awesome and almighty.'" All the voices blend together. "'Help us to understand and follow the path You have chosen for us. As athletes, let us compete in the image of Christ.'" Liam looks around. He doesn't even know what competing in the image of Christ means.

"'Heavenly Father, through You, all gifts come to us.'" Liam's throat tightens as he follows the words on the page. "'We give all praise and honor in Your name.'" Seth reads along next to him, and Pelke's loud voice echoes across the room. "'Help us to become champions for Jesus.'"

Liam stares at his paper. Image of Christ. Champions for Jesus. This doesn't feel right. He can't say these things just because everybody else is.

Pressure

XXX "Thanks for the chocolates, Kenz. They were great."

"Good. I'm so glad it's you. I'm dying to talk English."

He tosses dirty socks and boxers off his chair and sits down. "What are you doing?"

"Homework. And I'm sick of it. I'm sick of everything being in French." She sighs. "I have to work so hard to say the right words, and sometimes I know what I want to say, but I don't have the vocabulary, so I sound like a total idiot."

"I do that in English."

"Living with someone else's family is frustrating, too. Everybody says treat it like your own home, but it isn't mine. I have to adjust to their ways of doing things. They only talk to me in French, too, even though they all know English." She pauses. "I miss my own house. I miss my family. I miss you."

"I miss you, too, Kenz." Liam looks at her picture on his desk. "I wish you were here in my room."

"I wish you were holding me right now."

"I do, too." He scratches the back of his neck. "How are we going to handle fourteen and a half more weeks?"

"I don't know," she says. "Some days are harder than others."

"What are you wearing right now?"

"Why? I look terrible."

"You're so far away. Knowing would make you feel a little closer."

"My pink sweats and my coral Abercrombie tank top. Does that help?"

"Yeah. Is your hair pulled back?"

"No, it's down."

"Good." A semester feels way too long. Why couldn't she go for a week at spring break? "So what do you miss the most?"

"Turtle Blizzards from Dairy Queen."

"No. Really?"

"You, silly. I miss you."

"You can have both as soon as you get back." Excitement rushes through him, and he shifts his position.

"Yummy." She giggles. "How did your day go?"

"It was strange." Liam picks at a fingernail and tells her about the HAF meeting. "Some people seem sincere, but others, like Pelke, don't believe any of it and are only saying the words. I can't do that."

"Of course not," Mackenzie says.

"I'd feel like a fake." Liam stands. "And Coach leads prayers before every game and at halftime and expects us to lead them, too. It feels weird."

"What's the matter with prayer?"

"Nothing, but it's kind of a personal thing. I don't think Coach should be making us do it in the locker room."

"It sounds to me like you're worrying too much."

Liam looks out the window and doesn't respond. He's not worrying. Just trying to tell her what's going on. Why can't she see that?

"Liam." Mackenzie fills the silence. "I've got some bad news. My dad got my cell phone bill. It cost a ton. He's upset at how much we've been talking. He says I'm only supposed to use my phone to call them or for emergencies."

"What?" They haven't talked that much. Liam stares at the dried cornstalks standing in the snow.

"I can't call you for a month," she says.

"A month?"

"That's what my dad said."

Liam sits down on the bed and rubs his eyes.

"I'm sorry," Mackenzie says quietly. "Li, are you still there?"

"Yeah." He opens his eyes.

"Don't be mad at me. It's not my decision. I'll e-mail."

"It's not the same."

"I know," she says. "I'm frustrated, too. We'll just have to get through this month."

"I don't know if I can make it that long."

"I've got to go, Li. Dad will see this call on next month's bill. We'll figure something out. Bye, Li."

"Bye." Liam snaps his phone shut and pounds his fist on the bed.

XXX Saturday night, Liam's hands fly at the controls of NBA Live. He's up ninety-nine to ninety-eight and traps Seth at half-court. Seth twists and launches a wild shot.

"For the win," Seth shouts.

"No way," Liam hollers.

The ball swishes through the net.

"Yes! Yes! Yes!" Seth jumps up and down using the couch as a trampoline.

"I don't believe it." Liam tackles Seth and they fall to the carpet.

"Believe it, sucker." Seth turns him over and pins him.

The doorbell rings and Seth runs to get it.

"Good evening, Mr. Pizza Man. Let me introduce you to the Big Loser." He motions to Liam. "He's paying and he tips extremely well."

Liam pulls bills out of his wallet and gives them to the delivery guy.

Seth opens the box. "Pineapple and ham? Who'd ruin pizza by putting pineapple on it?"

"It's good," Liam says. "Try a piece."

"No chance." Seth grabs a pepperoni slice. "Don't let any of that pineapple get on my half."

Liam slurps his Pepsi. "That meeting at Drake's house. What did you think of it?"

"It was okay." Seth chews with his mouth open.

Liam wipes cheese off his chin. "We didn't do anything like that last year."

Seth leans forward. "Drake says it builds team unity and helps guys focus."

"I don't know about that." Liam shrugs. "Are you going again on Thursday?"

"Yeah. Drake says it's a plus for making varsity next year."

"Really?" Liam wipes a blob of sauce from his jeans. Since when is Seth talking so much with Drake?

Seth burps loudly. "This time, though, I'll bring my own doughnuts."

XXX "What are you doing?" Liam sits down across from Mom at the dining room table.

"Budget review. I have finance committee tomorrow morning." Lines crease her forehead as she studies papers. "We must have been out of our minds to schedule that first thing on Monday." She pets Dizzy, who snores in her lap.

"How's it look?" Liam picks up an eraser.

"I need to make more cuts." She circles a number with a red pencil. "Maybe I'll lay myself off. I could get back to my painting." She circles another number. "But somebody has college coming up, so I guess I have to keep plugging away. Do you have any more of those chocolates?"

"No, I finished them."

"Darn. I could really use one."

"Mom, remember when you asked about Coach Kloss?" Liam squeezes the eraser.

"Yes." She crosses out a line on her page.

"Well, he's kind of into religion."

"What do you mean?" She looks up.

"You know . . . prayers and stuff."

"What kind of prayers?" She sets her pencil down.

"He makes up his own prayers." Liam rolls the eraser around.

"Christian prayers? Does he mention Jesus?"

"Yeah, he talks about the Lord and doing His work. Then we always say the Our Father."

"I don't believe this. He can't be doing that in public school." Mom stands, dumping Dizzy to the floor. "He's a teacher whose salary is paid by taxpayers. He can practice any faith he wants, but he can't lead you kids in prayer at school."

Liam taps the eraser on the table. "That's kind of what I thought. Coach acts like everybody on the team is a Christian, but he doesn't know that. Not everybody at school is."

"Of course not." Mom's face flushes when she gets worked up. "Leah Braverman is on the girls' team and she's Jewish. How do you think she'd feel if her coach led Christian prayers?"

"Uncomfortable." Liam slouches in his chair.

"Of course. Separation of church and state is a fundamental American principle." She sits down directly across from him, and her eyes zero in. "What are you going to do about it?"

"I don't know." He shakes his head. "I just wanted to talk about it, not do something."

"Liam, it's wrong. When something is wrong, you have an obligation to take action."

Liam concentrates on the wood grain of the oak table. Suddenly, he feels in over his head. He's not like Mom. He's not looking for controversy.

Besides, he can't jeopardize his place on varsity.

His Call

XXX Monday morning, Liam arrives at school early and goes straight to the gym. JV players in street clothes are finishing up their one hundred free throws.

"Bergie, you're back," Seth calls out. "You missed us so much, you couldn't stay away?"

"Yeah, you especially." Liam blows Seth a kiss and the guys laugh.

"Sick." Seth drains a free throw. "Fifty-eight."

Liam leans against the Blazer Country mat behind Seth's hoop and watches guys shoot. It seems ages ago that he played with them.

"Fifty-nine." Seth hops around as the ball rolls around and drops in.

Coach G moves among the players, offering advice. He's a good coach — serious about winning but low-key in practice. Liam improved a lot playing for him.

Seth sinks another shot. "Sixty percent." He dances over

to Liam. "Hey, just because you're on varsity doesn't mean you can't come to our games."

"I know." Liam folds his arms.

"We're playing here Friday." Seth puts him in a head-lock. "Come support your boys."

"I'll try." Liam breaks free as guys head to the locker room to write down their percentages on the chart.

"Hey, Coach G." Liam holds out his hand.

"Hi, Liam." Coach G squeezes with a firm grip. He's got reddish-brown hair and a bushy mustache.

Liam picks up a loose ball and sets it in the cage. "Coach, I've got something I want to ask you."

"Shoot." Coach gathers two more balls and tosses them to Liam.

"When I played for Coach Cullen in ninth grade and for you on JV, we never prayed before games or talked about Jesus." Liam shoves the balls in.

"Yup."

"Now on varsity, we do."

"Yup." Coach G wheels the cage to the equipment

room and Liam trails after him. "Every coach does things his own way."

"Yeah, but why didn't you do it?"

"Kids come from different backgrounds and believe different things. Some kids don't believe much of anything." Coach G pushes the rack against the wall. "I have to work with kids where they are." He pulls out a key ring from his pocket.

"So you don't think prayer in the locker room is a good idea?"

"I didn't say that." Coach G locks the door and shakes the handle to make sure it's secure. "You need to talk with Coach Kloss about that. You're on varsity now. It's his call."

XXX At practice, Liam plants his feet against Drake, who's banging against him. Pelke passes the ball and Liam turns and shoots. Drake jumps and blocks it.

"Don't be looking for your shot, Bergie," Coach Kloss says. "We've got plenty of shooters on this team. Get the ball to them. Rebounding and defense, that's your job."

Liam hurries back on defense. "I've got yours." He slides over and slaps the ball off Nielsen's knee.

"Good help defense," Coach calls.

Liam passes the ball in. Pelke shoots a long jumper and Liam runs to the hoop for the rebound. The ball bounces off the rim and he leaps for it. He passes to Gund, who nails the jumper from the free throw line.

"Good board." Staley slaps Liam's hand.

"Drake, you can't give up easy rebounds like that," Coach shouts.

Liam runs downcourt with extra energy. It's a rush to anticipate where the ball will go. It's like seeing the future.

Coach blows his whistle. "Bonus situation. Hit both ends of the one and one." Coach shoots a free throw and hits all net. "If you miss your first one, run two laps around the gym. If you miss your second, one lap."

Liam looks at the other guys, who are catching their breath. Just what they need. Pressure free throws to end practice.

"We're in this as a team." Coach makes his second shot. "We're not leaving until everybody makes two in a row."

Liam grabs a ball, dribbles to the far hoop, and lines up his feet. He bounces the ball twice and shoots. The ball hits the front rim and rattles in.

Drake runs past. He must have missed his first shot. Liam goes to the line and eyes the hoop. He dribbles and shoots. Too hard. The ball clangs off the back rim. He leaves the ball bouncing and takes off running. Nielsen's ahead of him. He must have missed his, too. They're going to be here all night.

Liam runs back, picks up the ball, and toes the line. He doesn't want to be the last one. The ball is off to the right from the moment it leaves his hands. He runs hard on his two laps, passing Gund and Staley, who are sprawled out on the bleachers. They made their two in a row. That figures — they're the two best shooters on the team. Pelke jogs over to join them. He's not a great shooter, but he hits his free throws.

Liam finishes his second lap and picks up the ball. *Relax. Take your time.* He dribbles, exhales, and shoots. The ball hits the rim, rolls back, and drops in. One more.

"C'mon, Bergie. Finish it off," Staley shouts.

Liam lines up, feeling eyes on him. *Relax. Take your time.* He aims and shoots. *Swish* — the beautiful sound. He runs to the bleachers and pounds fists with Pelke and Staley.

Drake and Nielsen are still shooting and Liam exhales a long breath. It's better to watch than be watched. Drake makes his shot and raises his arms in triumph.

"You can do it, Nielsen." Staley claps.

Liam starts clapping, too. Staley's solid. As head of HAF, he doesn't just talk. He walks the walk.

Nielsen lines up and makes the first one.

"Big Man, Big Man," Pelke chants.

"Big Man, Big Man." Liam joins in with the others.

Nielsen buries the second and grins with embarrassment and relief.

XXX After getting dressed, Liam sits on the bench in the locker room and rubs the rash on his finger. Everybody else is gone.

What's Coach Kloss doing? Liam gets up and paces back and forth in front of the training room. Why is he taking so long?

He goes back to the bench and sits down. Suddenly, he feels dizzy, like the room is closing in on him. He grabs his coat and rushes out the back door. He takes a breath of cold air. He can talk to Coach some other time.

Wind whips snow around the dark parking lot as he turns on the Toyota and pops in a CD. He races out of the empty lot, and the orange warning light next to the gas gauge blinks on. He doesn't feel like getting gas in the cold.

He doesn't want to go home and have Mom question him either, so he stops at Subway. "Turkey sandwich on wheat with everything except onions and hot peppers, and two chocolate chip cookies." While he waits, he calls home and leaves a message. "I'm going to see Grandma. I'll be back later."

XXX The powerful disinfectant smell of the nursing home hits his nose as he opens the door. An old woman playing solitaire in the recreation room goes back to her cards when she doesn't recognize him. The TV blasts at full volume, but nobody is paying attention to it.

He comes to room 103. Elizabeth Bergstrom. That still looks strange. Most people call her Lizzie. She sits in the chair with her head down. "Hey, Grandma."

"Arlen?" She looks up.

"No, it's me. Liam."

"Arlen?"

"No, Liam." He moves closer. Maybe she was sleeping.

She peers through her glasses. "Liam? You look like Arlen."

He's tall and thin like Dad and he has his big nose, but that's about it. "I brought you a cookie." He holds up the bag. "Chocolate chip. Not homemade, but I thought you'd like it."

"I would." She looks at her tray. "They gave us JELL-O. JELL-O's not a real dessert."

"Definitely not." Liam unwraps the cookie and offers it to her.

"Thank you." She clicks off *Wheel of Fortune*. "How can they give away so much money on that show?"

Liam sits down and explains about advertising, sponsorship, and television ratings.

"I still don't understand where the money comes from." Grandma nibbles her cookie.

Liam laughs. "That's okay. I don't really understand it either." He wipes chocolate from his lips. "So, Grandma, did Dad tell you I'm on varsity basketball?"

"Yes. He did." She speaks slowly, like she's struggling to remember. She picks up her napkin and pats her mouth. "How are you doing?"

"The basketball part is going fine." Liam crumples the paper from the cookie and throws it in the trash. "There's something else I've got to talk to Coach about and I'm not sure how he'll react."

Grandma looks at him with her tired blue eyes. "I'm sure you'll do what's right."

XXX After the nursing home, Liam stops by the new gym at the Y. Dad says it was built when he was in high school, but everybody still calls it the new gym. Dad's warming up with his teammates. Some of them are teachers. Some are high school buddies who've stayed in Horizon. A couple of them are both.

"I thought we had a shot against West Branch." Mr. Mattson, Liam's eighth-grade math teacher, rolls in a layup. "But we didn't have anyone to stop Collinswood."

"Yes, we did." A left-hander wearing a sleeveless shirt shoots a jumper. "Darius Buckner. He would have slowed Collinswood down."

"I heard he's not coachable." Mattson bounces the ball.

"Maybe not by Kloss." Left-hander grabs a rebound. "Maybe it's time for a new coach."

"What do you mean?"

"Kloss can't lose talent like that in the middle of the season. What he's doing isn't working."

"Give me a break," Mattson says. "He's a good coach."

"We'll see." Left-hander nails another jumper. "If he doesn't get this group into the playoffs, he's not a good coach."

"Okay, fellas. Let's run." Dad steps between them.

Liam watches from the balcony. These guys take Horizon hoops seriously, but he's still surprised at such direct criticism of Coach Kloss. The guys on varsity might complain about their minutes, but they never question Coach's position. After all, he's the coach and he controls who plays and who doesn't.

"Liam played well." Mattson stands next to Dad at the free throw line. "He held his own in the second half."

"He's coming along." Dad drains a free throw.

Liam scrunches down in his seat so they don't see him listening.

"It's a big step up to varsity in the middle of the season, especially for a sophomore." Mattson banks a shot off the board as the ref blows his whistle.

Dad jumps for the opening tip and Mattson controls the ball. He passes it into the post. Dad dribbles once and shoots a right-handed sky hook that rolls in.

"Old school," Mattson calls. "They can't stop that."

Dad laughs as he runs back on defense. He catches sight of Liam and waves.

Liam gives him a thumbs up. That was a nice move, but nobody else is here to see it. The over-forty league doesn't get a lot of spectators. He rubs his eyes and tries to forget about the conversation he didn't have with Coach.

Or the one still to come.

Uncomfortable

XXX *Behnnnnnnnnnn.* Liam wakes to the annoying sound of his phone alarm buzzing on the dresser. He stumbles out of bed and shuts it off. It's way too early, but since he's out of bed, he's up. That's why he keeps it so far away.

He shuffles to his computer to see if Mackenzie has e-mailed. More penis-enlargement pills and Mr. Emerson Okambe offering five million dollars to open a bank account for him in the United States. Who's stupid enough to fall for that? Obviously someone is because they keep sending them. Nothing from Mackenzie. One more day and he'll e-mail her again.

He drags himself to the shower and lets the water heat up. He didn't sleep well. Turning and waking and checking the clock. Not being able to fall back to sleep. He's more tired now than when he went to bed.

After a breakfast of Cocoa Puffs, orange juice, and two strawberry Pop-Tarts, he heads outside to clean off the windshield while the car warms up. The ice feels glued on. He pushes down to a clear spot so he can work the edges.

Winter is the worst. Uncle Carl, Dad's brother, always says, "Come down to Tampa. Sun shining. Seventy degrees." Florida sounds very nice right now.

Snap. The blade on his scraper breaks. Liam takes his student ID out of his wallet and picks with that. The defroster has softened some of the ice, so he chips away with his tiny face watching him. It's too strange, so he flips it over.

In the car, the orange low-gas sign is still on. Why didn't he fill up last night? That would have been better than having to do it now. He pulls into Shirley's Gulp and Go and walks inside. Everything is credit card or cash up front now because people have been driving off without paying. He gets stuck at the register behind a couple in matching Arctic Cat jackets buying lottery tickets based on their grandchildren's birthdays.

"Callie's the sixth of July, not the ninth." The woman holds up six fingers.

"It's the ninth. Eight, nine." The guy's got a gravelly voice. "I always remember eight, nine for July ninth."

"Eight isn't the number for July. That's August and her birthday's in July, not August. It's July sixth."

Liam catches the eye of the pretty cashier with purple nail polish and slides his money forward.

Outside, he unscrews the cap and turns on the pump. He needs to hurry to have time to talk to Coach before first period.

XXX At school, Liam waits in the hall outside Coach's math room. Iris Cleary is talking to Coach about a make-up test. Liam rocks back and forth on his heels. She's taking forever.

What's he going to say anyway? What if he told Coach that he's uncomfortable with the prayers and HAF because he's not a Christian? Maybe he could say he was a Sikh. He went to school with Sikhs in Seattle. What would Coach say if he showed up for practice in shorts, shoes, and a turban?

He pulls at the red tie that's snug around his neck. Coach insists that they dress up for road games to give a good image of Horizon. Liam feels like he's choking and his feet pinch in his dress shoes. He can't wait any longer. There's not enough time now before the bell. He scrambles away down the hall.

English is as boring as ever. Mrs. Stabenow reads from her notes and drones on about symbolism in poetry like only she's smart enough to figure it out. He used to like reading when he was little, but there's nothing like being forced to read a bunch of boring books to take the fun out of it.

XXX After school, Liam walks into the locker room. The bus leaves for Tintah in half an hour, so Coach will probably be in his office getting ready for the game. Liam jams his fingers between his neck and tie to create some space. He's always hated ties. *Calm down. Relax.* He knocks on the door.

"Come in, Bergie." Coach pauses game film of Tintah and pulls newspapers off the metal folding chair. "What's on your mind?"

Liam takes a deep breath. "I'm really glad to be on varsity. I appreciate the opportunity."

"You earned it, Bergie." Coach looks at him like he knows this can't be the reason Liam's here. "When Jensrud got hurt, we needed another tall guy. Height is the one thing I can't coach."

Liam smiles. "I feel like I'm learning a lot."

"You are. You pay attention. You play hard. You're improving. That's all we ask. As a sophomore, of course, you have a lot to learn. And we need you to put some muscle on that frame for next year."

Liam nods. He's shaking all over, like he's fallen into an icy lake. "Coach, you said if we ever had anything we needed to talk about to come on down."

"That's right. My door is open." Coach leans back and spreads his arms. "What's on your mind?"

"Coach, I've never been on a team where we pray together before games . . . and I've been thinking about it."

Coach picks up a pen and clicks it. "You're a Christian, aren't you?"

"Yeah, I'm Catholic." Liam puts his hands on his knees to keep his feet from tapping.

Coach frowns. "Bergie, I'm surprised you're bringing this up."

"I'm not sure everybody is comfortable with it."

"No one has said anything to me." Coach clicks the pen again. "Has someone said something to you?"

"No." Liam looks down at the floor.

"Then it's only you. Are you comfortable with it?"

"I don't know." Liam remembers his conversation with Mom. "I'm not sure it's right in school."

"It's fine." Coach sets the pen down. "If you want, I'll check it out."

"Okay." Liam doesn't know what else to say. He concentrates on holding still.

"I respect you for coming to talk to me, Bergie. I'll look into it."

XXX The locker room at Tintah smells musty. Liam sits on a small plastic chair and pulls up his socks. He loosens his left foot by making the letters of the alphabet. When he went to physical therapy last year after spraining his ankle, they made him move it side to side thirty times and up and down thirty times. It was so boring, a lot of times he didn't finish.

Then one day he got a physical therapist with long blond hair who played basketball herself. She had him write the alphabet with his big toe. Once he got to C he felt like he couldn't stop until Z, and his foot got a good stretch. If he gets hurt again, he wouldn't mind seeing her.

"Tintah's tough at home." Coach Kloss stands in front of the chalkboard. Nobody else in the conference has a locker room so old they still have a chalkboard. He writes nine and seven, the team record, on the board. "This isn't acceptable." He taps a piece of chalk on the board. "It's not acceptable to me and it shouldn't be to you."

Liam knows the numbers too well. If he'd made those two free throws against Crosston, they'd be ten and six.

"Our goal since the start of the year has been to be the best-conditioned team in the conference." Coach throws the chalk on the floor. "We're going to go out and run Tintah into the ground. Are you ready to do what it takes to win?"

"Yesssss!" everyone shouts.

"Pelke, will you lead us in prayer?"

"Sure, Coach." Pelke folds his hands and looks serious. "Lord, we ask for Your guidance. Show us the path You've chosen for us and help us compete in the image of Christ."

Liam stares at him. Pelke doesn't believe any of this. He's just saying what Coach wants.

"Lord, help us to be victorious in Your name." Pelke catches Liam staring and winks.

"Thanks," Coach says. "Let's all say the Lord's Prayer."

"Our Father, who art in heaven, hallowed be Thy name . . ." Liam says the prayer with the others. Doesn't Coach see what a fake Pelke is?

XXX Tintah's terrible, and Horizon stretches the lead to nineteen in the second half. Both Drake and Nielsen have stayed out of foul trouble and played the whole game. On the bench, Liam fingers the HWJC band he remembered to wear tonight and presses his elbows into his knees. When he lifts them, they've made rising suns on his skin.

"Keep running the offense," Coach shouts. "Work the ball around."

Tintah's slow to rotate on defense, and Staley gets free. He's too good a shooter to leave open, and he buries the three-pointer.

Liam gets in for the final four minutes. That's a lot less time than last game. Is it because Drake and Nielsen played so well? Did Coach want them to run a whole game to improve their conditioning?

Or is Coach sending him a message?

Mackenzie's Spot

XXX By the time the bus gets back from Tintah, it's 11:30. Mom might still be up, and Liam doesn't want to talk to her about what happened with Coach, so he drives past Seth's house. The lights are off and Seth doesn't answer his phone. Because of his morning weight lifting, he's an early-to-bed guy lately. Liam winds down the back road to the gravel pit.

He gets out and looks at the stars. No moon tonight and no lights nearby, so the waves of the Milky Way are visible. Mr. Quist, Liam's seventh-grade science teacher, once said that there were more stars than individual grains of sand on all the beaches in the world. That seemed like such a far-out idea, but looking up now, it might be possible.

Liam spots the Big Dipper and follows it to the North Star. Always there, always in the north, always true north. He searches for the Little Dipper coming off the North Star. Those stars are tougher to identify with everything else so bright, but he looks closely and finds them.

Coach Kloss is hard to figure out. He told Liam to come down and talk anytime, but then he didn't seem very willing to listen or explain things. At least he said he'd check it out.

Liam walks past empty vodka bottles in a fire pit where kids have been partying. He ducks in among the tamarack trees, but the cold penetrates everything. He's not dressed warmly enough to be out here and his feet are tingling. He scrambles back down to the car, where the clock says 12:07. He drives out the shortcut, but the road is washed away. He has to back up and go out the other way.

XXX "Where have you been?" Mom's stretched out on the couch in her flannel robe with Dizzy curled up on top of her.

"Why are you still up?" Liam takes off his coat.

"I couldn't sleep." Mom marks her spot and closes her book. She sniffs, rubs her nose, and sneezes. Dizzy flies off her like she's been blasted out of a missile launcher.

"Bless you."

"Thanks." Mom takes a tissue from her pocket. "Why are you so late?"

"After we got back from Tintah, I wasn't ready to come home. I needed some time to think." Liam kicks off his dress shoes.

"You can't think here?"

"I needed some space, some time to myself."

"Did you talk to Coach Kloss today?" Mom pats the couch and Dizzy warily climbs back up.

"Yeah."

"What did he say?"

"That praying in the locker room is fine." Liam grabs grape juice from the fridge and pours himself a glass.

"It's not." Mom shakes her head.

"Coach said he'd check it out."

"With whom?"

"I don't know." Liam wipes grape juice from his lips.

"You didn't ask?"

"Coach said he'd take care of it."

"What does that mean?"

"I don't know, Mom." Liam looks at the clock on the microwave: 12:41. "Maybe it was a mistake to talk to him."

"It wasn't a mistake, Liam."

"We'll see." He climbs the stairs and unbuttons his shirt. She doesn't realize how hard it was for him to talk to Coach. She doesn't realize what he's risking. He only played four minutes tonight. She didn't even ask him about the game.

XXX The next morning, Liam turns on the computer to see if he has mail from Mackenzie. Finally. He clicks her name.

From: Mackenzie Kost

To: Liam Bergstrom

Date: February 2

Subject: intense

sweet liam,

so intense around here. sunday some friends took me over to montpellier. walked around awhile before we found a cozy little café. ate cerveau. afterward they told me what it was. calf brains! yuck. :-p the french eat all kinds of gross stuff! stayed late talking and drinking wine. btw my french is better when i drink! everyone says so. got up early to get back to school in time. jeanbaptiste drove

like a crazy man. jk he's really a good driver. everyone

here drives like a maniac. took a nap as soon as I got

back from school. went shopping today by myself and

bought a sexy black dress. ;-> tres paris. can't wait for

you to see it.

whats up with u? how's the team?

pix of my house and school and friends.

<3

lyl

x o x o kenz

He clicks open the pictures. An ancient-looking two-story house with no yard. The school's old, too — a brown building with huge trees in front. Her friends are three guys and two girls crowded onto a couch with five wine bottles on a table in front of them. The girls are thin and gorgeous and are smoking cigarettes. They're sitting in the guys' laps. The guys are good-looking, too. They look older, like they're in their twenties.

One of the guys has curly hair and a goatee. That must be Jean-Baptiste. It's pretty easy to figure out. He doesn't have a girl sitting in his lap.

That must be Mackenzie's spot.

XXX When Liam gets home from practice, Mom's jamming papers into her bag. "I've got some lobbying to do at the meeting tonight, and I'm late. Dad and I already ate. There's food in the fridge. Just heat it up." She grabs her coat. "And give Dizzy some clean water."

Liam picks up Dizzy's bowl. Bits of soggy food skim the surface. He dumps it in the sink, rinses it out, and runs fresh water.

Dad comes in from the garage holding a blue bottle. "Liam, do you need washer fluid in the Toyota?"

"I don't know."

"Let's check." Dad turns on the outside light.

"Can't we do it later?"

"No. When you have a car, you need to take care of it. Let's go."

Liam grabs his coat and slips on his Timberlands. Dad's

wearing a sweater. The cold doesn't seem to bother him. Maybe you develop immunity if you grow up with it.

He clicks the release and Dad lifts the hood. "Here, you do it." Dad gives him the bottle. "Check the level in that plastic tank. Does it need more?"

Liam bends down to look. "Yeah, it's way below the line."

"You won't believe it, but when I was a kid we had a car that didn't even have washer fluid."

"What did you do?" Liam pours the blue liquid carefully.

"You looked through the grime of the windshield the best you could. When it got so bad you couldn't see, you'd pull over, grab some snow, and rub it around on the windshield."

Liam snaps on the cap and gives the bottle back to Dad.

"Keep it," Dad says. "Put it in your trunk so you have it when you need it."

"Thanks." He wedges the bottle between the blanket, snow shovel, and emergency kit that Dad makes him keep in the car in the winter.

"I saw your grandma this morning," Dad says. "That was nice of you to visit."

"How was she doing?"

"Pretty good today. You're the only one of her grandchildren whom she sees regularly. It means more to her than you can imagine."

Liam jams his cold hands in his pockets. This is Dad's way of reminding him he should get over there more often.

"How about a quick game of H-O-R-S-E?" Dad goes to the hoop on the side of the driveway and pretends to shoot a layup.

"In the cold?"

"Come on, Liam. When I was your age we played outside. And it used to be a lot colder."

"My fingers are already numb. How about P-I-G?"

"H-O-R-S-E," Dad says. "Go get the ball."

Liam shuffles to the garage and picks up the ball. "My shot." He knocks down a jumper from the side. Dad matches that and then kills Liam with a couple of sky hooks.

Liam's hook shot falls short. "I never learned that shot."

"You should." Dad demonstrates the motion. "Nobody can block it."

Liam gets Dad to H-O-R on three corner jumpers, but then Dad switches to left-handed hooks to put Liam at H-O-R-S.

"One shot to finish it off." Dad stands with his back to the basket. "Watch this." He slams the ball into the ground and the ball hits the board and banks in. "No looking at the hoop. Make that."

"Pure luck." Liam lines up and tries to figure out how hard to bounce the cold ball. He blows on his right hand for warmth. He bounces the ball a few times and then slams it down like Dad did. He turns and sees that it's not nearly enough force. The ball lands in the snow.

"You still can't beat me." Dad raises his arms and does a goofy little dance.

XXX Inside, Liam goes to the fridge and unwraps the plate of chicken and mashed potatoes. "Dad, I had a talk with Coach Kloss yesterday." He presses the button on the microwave.

"Your mom mentioned that." Dad digs into a piece of pecan pie.

"What do *you* think?"

"It's fine that you talked with him. He shouldn't be leading prayers at school, but things are different here. You have to be patient. Things take time in Horizon."

"What if Coach says there isn't anything wrong with what he's doing?"

Dad takes another bite of pie. "Cross that bridge when you come to it."

Separation

XXX Liam gazes at the empty white box on his computer screen. He's written three e-mails to Mackenzie and deleted each one. Talking on the phone is so much easier than writing. With writing, everything that's wrong stares right back at you.

He wants to sound cool, like the picture of her friends doesn't bother him. It does, though, and that seeps into his words like blood into a bandage.

From: Liam Bergstrom

To: Mackenzie Kost

Date: February 2

Subject: The Same

Kenz,

Finally an email from you. I couldn't figure out what happened. Everything here is the same. School's the same. Boring. Looks like you're having more fun there.

The team is up and down. Tomorrow we play at Delavan. I know you can't use your host family's phone, but what if you got a calling card. Then you could call me. I miss talking with you.

Sweethearts Ball is in two weeks. :-< Too sad without you.

<3

Liam

x o x o x o x o

He types Xs and Os at the bottom for hugs and kisses, because Mackenzie likes that kind of stuff, and rereads the message. It's lame, but he's sick of trying to get the words right. He hits SEND and the message zips around the world.

He Googles Arles and up pops a series of pictures of Mackenzie's town. An old man rides a bike while carrying a baguette. Tourists line up outside a Roman coliseum. Couples stroll arm in arm on a path along the Rhône River. Liam examines each picture closely as if he might spot Mackenzie with Jean-Baptiste. What is he doing? Pathetic.

He goes to NBA.com and watches highlights of last night's games. The pros make going to the hoop look so easy. It's as if they walk on air, as if they're not bound by gravity.

Liam's phone rings and he grabs it.

"What are you doing?" Seth asks.

"Watching some videos on NBA.com."

"Yeah, I'm sure that's what you're watching." Seth laughs. "What have you been up to? I've hardly seen you this week."

"Stuff." Liam scratches his head. "I talked with Coach Kloss yesterday about those prayers."

"Why?"

"I don't like being pressured to be a champion of Jesus."

"So what. It's not that big a deal," Seth says. "You're on varsity as a sophomore. Do you have any idea how many people would kill for that?"

"Yeah. I'm talking to one of them."

"Are you coming to our JV game on Friday?"

"Yeah. I'll be there."

"What about HAF tomorrow?"

"I don't know."

"What are you? An idiot?" Seth shouts and Liam holds the phone away from his ear. "You have to do these things to be on varsity. Quit making things difficult."

Liam snaps his phone shut. He doesn't need a lecture from Seth. Downstairs, he hears Mom coming in from the garage. He's still hungry, so he goes down to see what else he can find.

"James Buckner from the college gave a superb presentation that wowed the whole committee. Nine to zero. I thought we might have a fight, but it went through unanimously. For the first time ever, we're going to feature a high school student in the spring exhibition."

"Congratulations, Kate." Dad sets down a pack of lightbulbs and gives her a kiss.

"Who's the student?" Liam cuts a brownie from the pan and sits at the table.

"Leah Braverman. Professor Buckner says her work deserves the honor. He says age is an artificial barrier in the face of such talent."

"Is that Darius's dad?" Liam takes a huge bite.

"Yes. I told him I was angry at how Darius had been treated on the basketball team." She fills the kettle and turns on the burner. "Who wants a cup of tea?"

"I do," Dad says. "But first I have to change the light in the bathroom." He pulls a bulb out of the pack.

"Liam, do you want anything hot?" Mom unwraps two apple-cinnamon tea bags.

"No thanks." He cuts another brownie.

Mom turns to him. "How about you? What's happening with Coach Kloss?"

"I'm waiting to see what he says." Liam licks chocolate off his fingers.

"Listen, I've got a lawyer on my board, Kendra Gronquist. I could talk to her about filing a complaint with the superintendent." The kettle whistles and Mom grabs it.

"Mom, I'm not filing a complaint. Let me handle this. You don't go to practice. You don't have to worry about playing time or getting along with Coach."

She pours hot water into the mugs. "Well, it's simply my

opinion, but I don't think he's going to change without pressure."

"Let me take care of it."

"I was only making a suggestion." She sets the kettle back on the stove.

"I don't want any suggestions. You're always making suggestions. 'Read this. Study that. Prepare for the PSAT. Get into a good college.'" His throat tightens.

Dad comes in and takes his mug.

"Let me be." Liam stands up.

"Listen, Liam." Mom turns to face him. "The reason I push you is because you've got gifts. You're bright. You're compassionate. You have ability."

Liam walks away from her. Dad's standing right there. Why doesn't he say something?

"And with gifts come responsibility." Mom raises her voice. "You have a responsibility to stand up for what's right."

"You're not listening, Mom. I need to do this my way, not your way." He slides on his boots and pulls his coat from the closet.

"Where are you going, Liam?"

He grabs his keys.

"What are you doing?"

He opens the door and the cold air rushes in.

"Don't leave like that," Mom shouts.

"Let him go, Kate," Dad says. "Let him go."

Fake

XXX In the locker room before the game at Delavan, Liam yawns as he pulls his red jersey over his winter-white body. Usually the adrenaline's pumping, but after driving around last night and getting up early for HAF, he's dragging.

Coach catches his eye and waves him over. Liam's heart-beat quickens. Is somebody sick? Is he going to start?

"You ready to rebound?" Coach rubs his palms.

"Yes."

"Good." Coach puts his hands on Liam's shoulders. "Bergie, I checked out our prayers with a couple of people. They said it's fine." His breath smells of mouthwash. "Nothing to worry about. You can focus on the game."

Who did Coach ask? Probably people he knew would agree with him.

Coach looks him in the eye. "Bergie, I'd like you to lead the prayer tonight."

Liam takes a step back. "Okay." Is this a test? What

should he say? He can't pull a Pelke and ask God for a win. God probably has one or two more important things to deal with than Horizon basketball.

"Everyone gather round." Coach motions to Liam. "Bergie is going to lead the prayer."

Liam folds his hands. "God, we ask for Your protection. We ask that . . . You guide us." He looks over at Coach, who nods to encourage him. His prayer is too general. It needs to be more specific, more about Jesus.

"Lord, help us to play well. Help us to do Your work . . . as we take the court. . . . Help us . . . help us to compete in the image of Christ."

"Thanks, Bergie." Coach smiles. "Let's all say the Lord's Prayer."

"Our Father, who art in heaven." Liam looks down at his HWJC band and prays along. He caved in. Just like Pelke, he said what Coach wanted. He's a fake, too.

XXX At the start of the second half, Nielsen picks up a quick foul guarding the Delavan center.

"Don't reach for the ball," Coach pleads. "How many times do I have to tell you? Get good position and keep your arms up." He looks down the bench. "Bergie, go in for Nielsen."

Liam wipes his hands on the soles of his shoes as he stands next to fifty-four. He's massive, with dark sideburns and a mustache. On the shot, Liam keeps a body on him, but fifty-four pushes back like a football player. He bangs around like Seth, and Liam struggles to grab the rebound.

"Here, Bergie." Staley comes back for the ball.

On offense, Liam sets a screen and Pelke cuts off it. Fifty-four jumps out on the switch, and Liam has a smaller guy on him. He goes to the hoop, but doesn't raise his hand to call for the ball. Pelke slides to the corner and knocks down a jumper.

At the next whistle, Nielsen comes back in and Liam takes a seat. Horizon plays tight man-to-man defense, and Delavan launches up shots in frustration. Drake and Nielsen grab long rebounds and Staley and Gund cherry-pick downcourt for easy hoops. Pelke hits two more jumpers. He's locked in and having a great game.

Horizon pulls ahead by fifteen, and Liam waits for Coach to put him back in. Four other subs go in first. Finally, with three minutes left, he goes in. Garbage time. The game's already decided.

XXX Driving home from school Friday, Liam sees a familiar form in a light blue, puffy coat. It's Darius, carrying a basketball.

Liam turns right at the next corner and drives back around the block. Despite what Darius says, it must be hard for him not to be on the team, to be out looking for a game on his own.

"Where are you going?" Liam leans over.

"The B-CAB."

"Where?"

"The Borton College Athletic Building," Darius says.

"Hop in. I go right by there." Liam opens the door.

Darius climbs in and Liam expects him to say thanks, but he holds the basketball on his lap and looks straight ahead. Liam waits for two cars to pass before he pulls out. "The team's not the same without you."

"I know."

They drive awhile in silence and Liam remembers how hard it was to fit in when he moved here. He can't imagine what it's like for Darius. "How are you liking Horizon?"

"I hate it," Darius says quietly. "Dad likes his job and Mom's happy to be out of Chicago, but I hate it."

Liam notices Darius's earring catching the light. Moving in high school is probably even worse than moving in middle school.

"It's a bad town to be black in," Darius says.

Liam thinks of Darius surrounded by a sea of white faces at school. "Guess what?"

"What?" Darius looks over.

"It's a bad town to be white in."

Darius breaks into a smile and he laughs deeply. "I'll remember that."

Liam pulls up to the heavily salted sidewalk in front of the Athletic Building. "Who are you playing with?"

"Nobody." Darius gets out. "I need to work on my threes."

"See you at school," Liam calls as Darius shuts the door. He shifts into drive. Mom was right about one thing: The team did treat Darius badly. And what did *he* do? He didn't stand up for Darius when those guys said he was selfish. He didn't stand up for him when Pelke called him the gay gunner. Nobody stood up for him.

XXX zzzzzttttttmmmmpppp Dizzy taps on keys as she crosses Liam's keyboard. "Get down." He pushes her aside.

Mom says the prayers are wrong and Dad says Coach shouldn't be leading them. But Coach Kloss says it's fine, nothing to worry about. Liam clicks on a link. After feeling like a fake yesterday, he needs his own information.

The American Civil Liberties Union site has some stuff on separation of church and state and a link for contact information. He clicks and a phone number for the state office comes up. Maybe it would be easier to talk to someone. He could call without giving his name. He digs around in his backpack for his phone.

"Thank you for calling the ACLU. For legal assistance, press one."

He punches the number.

"If you wish to request legal assistance, you must do so in writing. Our review committee will review your request to determine whether we can offer you legal assistance. Please send us a summary of your situation. If you have supporting documents that you would like us to review, please make copies and send them to us. Do not send original documents or your original copies of documents."

Liam hangs up. That's way too complicated. He goes back to the search page and picks another link: Americans United for Separation of Church and State. It's worth a try. He scrolls down and at the bottom is a number. Probably another voice mail.

"Hello, Americans United for Separation of Church and State," a woman answers. "This is Megan."

"Oh. I didn't expect a . . . person. A . . . real, live person."

"Yes, I'm alive. Can I help you?"

"I have a question. About prayer in school."

"Yes."

"Can a high school coach lead prayers in the locker room before basketball games?"

"Is it a public school?"

"Yes." Dizzy pads over and plops in his lap.

"No, the law is clear on that. A coach can't lead such prayers."

"Are you sure?"

"Positive," she says. "I can pull up a case for you. Hang on a second."

This is what he needs, somebody who knows what she's talking about. He doesn't have to rely on Coach's word.

"Here it is," Megan says. *"Doe versus Duncanville Independent School District.* The court found unconstitutional a basketball coach's practice of leading and participating in prayers with the junior high and high school teams before games, in the locker room, and after games."

That's exactly the situation at Horizon. Liam bookmarks the Americans United page.

Megan keeps reading. "Among the reasons that team prayer accompanying sporting events at public institutions has been held to be unconstitutional is the fact that attendance at games is not voluntary for members of the team. In

Doe versus Duncanville, the Fifth Circuit ruled that coach-led prayer would pressure some students to participate in a religious act that they objected to."

"Wow." Liam stands up from his desk.

"Your coach leading prayers is a violation of the Establishment Clause of the First Amendment," Megan says. "Public school coaches cannot promote religion to their teams. Would you like us to send a letter to your school?"

"No! No! I'm only getting information. I'm doing research."

"That's fine," Megan says. "Feel free to call if you have other questions or if there is anything I can do to help."

"Thanks." Liam closes his phone. Sounds like Mom is right. Which means Coach is wrong.

XXX Liam pulls two slices of white bread from the package and places them in the toaster. Mom's got an opening tonight and Dad's helping her set up, so he has to get his own dinner.

He opens the peanut butter jar. Megan didn't have any

doubts about it. Liam found the information easily enough. Coach could, too. Maybe he doesn't want to. Maybe he knows and is lying. Liam grabs the spoon in the pan to stir the eggs.

"Yowwwwwwww." His right index finger and thumb burn. He rushes to the sink and turns on cold water. He opens the freezer and grabs an ice pack, but remembers something about not shocking the skin. He hurries back to the sink and runs warm water to stop the burning, while he hops around like he's on hot coals.

He smells something burning. He races over and pops up the toast and blasts the fan on high. The last thing he needs is the smoke detector going off. He turns off the burner and examines the spoon. The black plastic handle has melted. That's what burned him. That spoon's for salad, not cooking. What an idiot. He dumps the eggs, toast, and spoon in the trash and takes it out to the garbage to hide the evidence.

He examines the bright red spots of the burn. A small spot on his thumb and a mark about the size of a dime on his finger. He washes them thoroughly and wraps two Band-Aids tightly to keep the area clean. It's his right hand — his shooting hand.

He dips a finger in the peanut butter. He's still hungry.

XXX That night at the JV game, Liam sits alone on the bleachers behind the bench. Seth spins to the hoop for the opening basket. Strong move. They were practicing that together a month ago. Liam shakes popcorn into his mouth as he watches the team play their matchup zone. The guys look good.

"Seth, rotate to the middle," Coach G calls out.

Liam presses lightly on the Band-Aid. The burn really hurts. Using that spoon was major-league stupid.

Seth bumps a guy with his hip and blocks the shot.

"Monster defense," Liam calls, and Seth looks over and grins.

If Liam were still on JV, he'd play most of the game, rather than sit on the varsity bench. He wouldn't have to worry about team prayers, or getting enough minutes, or talking to Coach Kloss. But it's too late now. He can't go back.

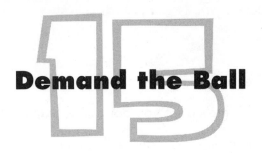

Demand the Ball

XXX "Great game against Delavan. You couldn't miss." Liam adds a box of Adidas to Pelke's pile at the store on Saturday.

"I haven't washed my hand since," Pelke says.

"I guess I won't shake it, then." Liam holds up a single Reebok.

"Maybe you should." Pelke tosses him the missing shoe. "You could use some of my touch. Works with hoops. Works with girls. I'm happy to share."

"Thanks." Liam boxes up the shoes and slides them into their slot. "Hey, you remember when I asked you about HAF?"

"Yeah."

"I found out Coach isn't supposed to be leading prayers in the locker room."

"What?" Pelke squints.

"I talked to someone about it."

Pelke beckons Liam over. "Listen, Bergstrom. You're a sophomore. There's a lot you don't understand. I'll give you a piece of advice. If you want to play on this team, you need to leave that stuff alone."

"What if Coach is wrong?" Liam turns his head away from the scent of Pelke's cologne.

"That's not the issue." Pelke pokes Liam in the chest. "Go along. Get along. Got it?"

Liam steps back. "What if I don't want to be fake about it?"

Pelke snorts. "It's not fake. It's how you get by. People do that every day."

"Not everyone does."

"What's the matter with you sophomores? You're acting like Buckner. He thought he was smarter than everyone else, too. Look where that got him."

The entrance bell rings and a short guy wearing glasses and a frown walks in.

"Hi, can I help you?" Pelke switches to his salesman voice.

Liam presses his two Band-Aids together. He should have

known better than to bring it up. Pelke doesn't care about anything other than his starting position.

The bell rings again and Iris Cleary goes straight to the women's section and examines a New Balance high-top.

"Hey, Iris, can I help you?"

"Do you have this in a ten?" She holds up the black shoe.

"Let me check." Liam looks at the code number. He sorts quickly through the boxes in back and finds the right one.

Iris sits on the bench and takes off her coat. She's wearing blue jeans and a gray T-shirt that says CLEAN THE GLASS with a cartoon of a girl soaring for a rebound.

"I like your shirt." Liam offers her the box.

"Thanks." She unties her Nikes.

"My job is to rebound." Liam isn't sure what to do with his hands so he holds them behind his back.

"Mine, too." Iris slips on the new shoes. "But Jack's on me to do more on offense, to be more assertive."

"Coach Kloss never says that to me." Liam laughs. He watches her arms as she laces up the shoes. She looks strong.

"How do you like the shoes?"

"I wonder if they're too big."

"Let me see." Liam uses his left hand to touch her toes through the leather. "That feels good." He checks the other foot. "That feels good, too."

"You think so?"

"Yeah, we don't have a nine and a half. You'd have to go all the way down to nine and that would be too small."

"I like how they look." She pivots back and forth.

"How do they feel?" Liam breathes in her fresh smell of soap and shampoo.

"Good, but I need to break them in." She notices his Band-Aids. "What did you do?"

"I was playing with fire."

"Be careful next time."

"How tall are you?" Liam stands next to her and realizes it sounds kind of personal.

"Five-twelve."

"Six feet? You're six feet tall?"

"Five-twelve." Iris smiles and her blue eyes sparkle.

XXX After work, Liam stops by the nursing home to see Grandma.

"Arlen?"

"No, it's me. Liam."

"Carl?"

"No, Liam," he says loudly.

"Oh, Liam." Grandma's lying on top of the bed in her clothes.

"Can I get you anything, Grandma?" Maybe he interrupted her nap.

"No."

"How about some fresh water?"

"Loverly," she says slowly.

He dumps out the old water. He's always liked the way Grandma says "loverly." He runs cold water and fills the glass.

"Here you go." He puts it on her tray and sits down in the recliner he and Dad brought over to make the room feel homier.

"Hur mår du?"

"What?"

"Jag kan bara svenska."

"Grandma, I don't speak Swedish. You know that. You have to use English." She looks at him as if she hears his voice but doesn't understand what he's saying. Sometimes she goes back to Swedish, the language she first spoke as a girl in Horizon. Her eyes shut and her head sinks forward.

Will she sleep for a few seconds or a couple of hours? He wonders if he should stay or go, and he deeply misses the way Grandma used to be.

XXX Saturday night, Liam bounces the ball on the court of the old gym at the Y. The wood here has darkened to a rich color from all the coats of varnish. The lights aren't as bright as the new gym's, and there's no track above for joggers to run around in circles. This gym reminds him of the one in Seattle where he first played in a league when he was seven. What was that team called? Panthers, Penguins, something with P. They wore black shirts. Pirates, that's it. Liam raced up and down the floor that first game, and that's pretty much all they did since nobody knew anything about offense or defense.

Liam made a basket in the second game. The rebound came off the left side of the hoop. He grabbed it and shot. The ball hit the board and banked in. A basket. Mom and Dad cheered, and he wanted to do it again and again and again.

He shoots a bank shot from ten feet. The bandages on his thumb and finger don't bother his shot much. The ball bounces off the board, rattles the front of the rim, and drops through. For his next shot, he aims lower on the board. The ball hits the glass exactly where he wants and falls into the net. Going to the court by himself is his escape. It's always been a refuge from problems with his parents, problems with girls, problems with school. He can go into a trance here. Shoot, rebound, shoot, rebound, shoot.

Liam stakes out the spots for Around the World. He used to play this with Dad in the driveway of the old house. Dad would pick the names of countries and call them out as they went around the court. He banks a shot off the board in Samoa. Dad always used the board for that shot, too.

Dad went net from Thailand, and Liam nails that one. He misses his first free throw from Oman, but takes his "chance" and hits the second. He eyes the hoop from Kenya at the top of the arc. This is the farthest shot and beyond his normal range, but he's practiced it hundreds of times because it's the key to Around the World.

He exhales, jumps, and launches the shot. The ball floats toward the hoop and drops in. Yes. That burst of satisfaction shoots through him. He knocks down shots in Ghana, Italy, and Belize, and then retraces his route to get home.

By the time Liam was fourteen, he could beat Dad one-on-one, but Dad always held his own in H-O-R-S-E and Around the World. "Concentrate on each shot," Dad used to say. "Don't replay your last shot or get ahead of yourself to the next one. Concentrate on what's happening now." Liam hears shoes squeaking behind him and notices Leah Braverman and Iris Cleary at another hoop.

"Establish position on the block with the defender sealed behind you." Leah demonstrates. "Raise your arm and demand the ball."

Liam swishes his shot from Kenya. Did they see that? Leah is here on a Saturday night, a senior working with a sophomore. Drake or Pelke would never do that with him.

He lines up his free throw from Oman. *Relax. Concentrate on what's happening now.* He shoots and is afraid it's short, but the ball catches the rim, bounces up, and drops in.

Nothing but net from Thailand. Two more shots and he's finished. Then he'll go down and say hello. He shoots and misses from Samoa. Too hard. *Don't think about talking to Leah and Iris. Concentrate on what's happening now.* He bounces the ball before shooting. If he misses here, he has to start all over. He exhales, aims for the backboard, hits it cleanly, and the shot drops through the net.

He banks in his layup at home for the win, grabs the ball, and walks to the other end. Why's he nervous about saying hello?

"Turn fast," Leah says. "If the turn is too deliberate, it gives the defender time to block the shot. Remember how Shea does it? Strong, decisive moves."

Iris catches the pass, turns quickly, and shoots.

"Nice move," Liam says from the top of the key. "How are the shoes?"

"Great." Iris lifts one up and flexes her ankle. "They fit fine with two pairs of socks."

"What are you practicing?"

"Entry passes and low-post moves." Leah retrieves the bouncing ball.

"But you win by twenty points every game, don't you?"

"That's regular season. Four weeks to the playoffs. That's a whole different ball game. Jack asked each of us to pick one aspect of our game to improve. I picked decision making. Iris picked demanding the ball."

Liam scratches his head. Demanding the ball sounds kind of selfish. That doesn't sound like Iris.

"But I shouldn't be speaking for Iris." Leah spins the ball on her finger. "That's poor decision making."

"How did you pick demanding the ball?" Liam turns to Iris, who's wearing long black shorts and a tight sleeveless T-shirt. She looks good.

"We have so many shooters, and like I told you,

sometimes I focus so much on rebounding that I forget about my shot. Jack wants me to shoot more, and to do that, I have to ask for the ball."

"Not ask," Leah interrupts. "You have to demand it."

Liam cradles his ball in his arms. She's tentative on offense. He and Iris struggle with some of the same things.

"We've got to get back to work." Leah walks to the wing.

"Have a good practice." He'd like to watch more of Iris's moves, but to stand here by himself would look strange.

"Thanks, Liam." Iris waves as Leah whips a bounce pass into the post. Iris turns and shoots.

"That's the way," Leah says. "Demand the ball and go strong."

That Bridge

XXX The next morning the world is outlined in white. Heavy snow clings to tree branches and weighs them down. Liam digs his shovel into the five inches that fell during the night and starts to clear a path. Thank God the sidewalk is short and Dad has someone who plows the driveway. If he had to shovel all that, he'd be out here until spring.

He throws wet snow in front of the bay window. Mom planted tulip bulbs there last fall, and she insists they stay covered to provide insulation against the cold. Liam looks at the frozen basketball hoop where Dad beat him in H-O-R-S-E. Putting the hoop up was one of the first things Dad did when they moved here.

Liam scrapes the plastic blade of the shovel against the concrete. "Cross that bridge when you come to it." That's what Dad said. He's been at that bridge since Thursday when Coach Kloss told him the prayers were okay. Now he's got to figure out how to cross.

The easiest option would be to do nothing. But that would be chickening out. It wouldn't be crossing the bridge; it would be turning around and going home. Besides, Mom's going to keep asking him what's going on, and he can't tell her Coach is still checking it out. He could go back and tell Coach what he's discovered. But Coach wasn't straight with him last time. Why would he be now?

Liam pounds his shovel on the walk to get the sticky snow off. What about Principal Craney? Could Liam ask him? Craney would say he'd look into it and that would take forever. Besides, he and Coach Kloss are friends. He'd say everything was fine, just like Coach did.

XXX "Pass me the Pringles." Seth licks the last crumbs of Doritos from the inside of the bag as the Suns run up the score on the Lakers.

"Jalapeño or Sour Cream & Onion?" Liam stretches out on the couch in his basement.

"Both." Seth rips a fart that sounds like a chain saw.

"Geez." Liam drops the cans on the couch and squeezes his nose.

"I can't help it," Seth says. "Cool Ranch Doritos make me fart. It doesn't happen with Nacho Cheese or any other flavors."

"No more Cool Ranch ever again." Liam grabs his Dr Pepper and takes a swig. "Seth, I found out some more about those prayers."

"Why is that such a big deal to you?" Seth rolls his eyes.

"Coach Kloss is lying about it."

"How do you know?"

"I did some research. Coaches aren't supposed to be doing that in school." Liam rubs an itch on his ankle with his foot. "And there's something about the way he put his hands on my shoulders and said, 'Don't worry about it.' He knows and he wants me to shut up."

"And why can't you do that?" Seth mutters.

"Because he's lying. Coach G never lies to us. How do you trust a coach who lies to you?"

Seth balances a mound of sour cream on a chip and jams it into his mouth. "How come nobody else has complained?"

"I don't know." Liam tears open a package of Oreos, takes one, and passes them.

"So why do you have to be the hero?" Seth takes three.

"I'm not trying to be a hero." Liam unscrews the top. "I don't like being lied to." He looks at the halves of cookie. "And nobody else wants to do anything about it."

"Let it be." Seth waves him off. "Don't screw things up. Why can't you listen to me?"

"I am listening." Liam scrapes his finger across the frosting and licks it. "But I have to decide for myself."

XXX As he opens his e-mail on Monday, Liam looks for something from Mackenzie. But again, there's nothing.

He could send her another one, but he doesn't want to seem desperate. He doesn't want to beg for attention. She never even replied about getting a calling card. She feels farther away than ever.

He sits and looks out the window. Coach Kloss lied to him. He said, "If you ever have anything you want to talk about, come on down." But then he lied. Liam rolls his neck to loosen the muscles. By lying to him, Kloss disrespected him.

So what's he going to do about it? He could let it be, like Seth told him to. Or he could do something dramatic like Darius did. But he's not Seth and he's not Darius. He's got to be himself.

On the court when he's boxed out, he has options. He can slide or spin or push to get free. He's got to create some space now. He turns back to the computer. He knows who to call.

XXX "Americans United for Separation of Church and State. This is Megan."

"Hi, I talked with you last week. I'm the one whose coach was leading prayers in the locker room."

"Which one? I've had a few of those lately."

"High school basketball. I was surprised to get a real, live person."

"Now I remember," Megan says with a laugh.

"My coach is leading prayers before games and he says it's fine." Liam plays with a rubber band.

"Coaches often say that without checking the law."

"What would be the next step?"

"We would have a lawyer send a letter to your school saying that the coach is leading team prayers, which courts have consistently said is unconstitutional, and ask them to inform us how they plan to ensure that the coach no longer leads religious activity with his team."

"Do you do that a lot? Send letters, I mean?" Liam snaps the band and it bounces off his computer screen.

"Every day."

"Who would the letter go to?"

"The principal and the superintendent of schools."

"Would they be told who contacted you?"

"No, we don't specify that," Megan says firmly. "We don't want you to get in trouble for doing what's right."

Liam turns in his chair and stares out the window at the gray sky. All the snow that coated the branches yesterday has fallen off. It's up to him.

"Hello. Are you still there?"

"I'm here." Liam stands up. He's on the other side of the bridge now. "I know what I want to do." He paces back and forth. "I want the letter sent." It's exciting to decide. Exciting, but scary.

XXX During the second half of the game at Clasco, Liam's thoughts jump around as he watches the action on the floor. Megan said they didn't need to use his name, but it won't be hard for Coach to figure it out.

It's odd sitting on the bench knowing someone in Washington, D.C., is writing a letter about Coach Kloss. Liam's done something that nobody else on the team knows about, something that they wouldn't agree with.

The pep band plays loudly to fire up the crowd. Most bands, including Horizon's, leave after halftime, but this one looks like they stay for the whole game. Maybe there isn't anything else to do in Clasco on a snowy February night.

"Bergie." Liam's brought back by Coach's voice. "Get in for Nielsen."

Liam rips off his warm-ups.

"We're getting killed on the boards," Coach says. "Grab some rebounds."

Liam checks in and jogs onto the court when the horn blows.

"You've got fifty-one." Nielsen slaps his hand.

Liam lines up next to fifty-one, who's a stocky guy with glasses. Liam has about two inches on him. The Clasco guard shoots his free throw, and Liam leans back to seal fifty-one. Liam fights to hold his position and the ball rolls off the rim. He taps it over to Drake. This guy is tough. No wonder Nielsen was having trouble.

When Liam sets up on offense, fifty-one uses his butt and hip to force him off the block. Liam pushes back, then pivots to set a screen for Pelke. Fifty-one sticks right with him. Back and forth they go, pushing and shoving. The refs aren't calling much, so Liam digs in to hold his ground. Basketball's a team game, but when a guy challenges you, it's important to step up.

Liam pushes for position and tips the ball in for a basket.

"That's the way to hustle." Coach claps.

Fifty-one calls for the ball on a post up. He throws an elbow against Liam's chest and gets called for the foul.

"Red ball." The referee points.

"Way to battle." Staley pulls Liam up.

On offense, Liam keeps moving so he's difficult to box out. He squeezes past fifty-one, times his jump, and rips another rebound. He passes to Drake, who takes it hard to the hoop.

"Good work," Drake says.

"Nice finish." Liam runs downcourt with Drake. How strange. After having the letter sent, he feels more relaxed on the court.

Maybe it's the calm before the storm.

You Owe Him

XXX When Liam gets home from school on Wednesday, Dad's gluing feathers on a paper plate at the dining room table.

"What's that?"

"Ouuu. Ouuu." Dad holds up an owl mask in front of his face.

"That's an improvement, Dad."

"Whooooo are yooooou to talk?" He pulls a feather off his ear. "The kids are going to go nuts for these."

Liam sits down. Sometimes it's strange to have a dad who's a kindergarten teacher. "Dad, I've got something to tell you."

"What?"

"Remember when I told you about Coach leading prayers at school?"

"Yes." Dad glues the loose feather down.

"I called a woman in Washington, Megan, who said

what Coach is doing is wrong. It's unconstitutional. She sent a letter to Principal Craney about it."

"Slow down." Dad holds out his palms. "Who is Megan?"

"She works for Americans United for Separation of Church and State."

"You did this on your own?" Dad frowns.

"Not on my own. Megan helped."

"I understand that, but who told you to call her? Your mom?"

"No. I did it."

"Why didn't you tell me you were thinking about this?"

"I'm the one on the team." Liam raises his voice. "I needed to do it."

"Oh, Liam." Dad rubs his forehead. "This is going to create a mess. People have strong feelings on this issue."

Liam squeezes his hands under the table.

"You worked so hard to make varsity. You've been playing well and contributing to the team." Dad shakes his head. "What's going to happen now?"

"I don't know." Liam stands up.

"Have you told Coach Kloss about the letter?"

"No."

"You owe him that."

"Why?" Liam scowls.

"Because he's your coach. He needs to know what's coming."

"You and Mom always tell me to stand up for what I believe. Then I do, and you're still disappointed."

"It's more complicated than that, Liam."

"I don't think so." He stomps upstairs.

XXX When Liam checks e-mail, he's thrilled to see Mackenzie's name. It's about time.

From: Mackenzie Kost

To: Liam Bergstrom

Date: February 9

Subject: crazy busy

liam,

crazy busy. last weekend went to avignon. u know the song sur le pont d'avignon? sur le pont d'avignon, on y danse, tout en rond. fyi it means on the bridge in avignon, everyone is dancing in a circle. did that saturday. sang the song on the bridge and everyone danced crazy together. almost fell off. lol! went shopping in the old center of town and bought a tiny leather purse. cute. almost walked out of the store without paying but the shop owner chased after us. :-)

what are u doin? how is horizon? i feel so out of it here. c'est la vie.

<3

lyl

kenz

x o x o

She is so out of it. Telling him about some stupid song and showing off her French. She's got money for a purse, but not for a calling card. The whole thing sucks, and he doesn't feel like writing back.

He hears the garage door opening and then the mumble of voices in the kitchen. Dad's probably telling Mom what happened. He clicks on YouTube and watches a girl taking off her clothes while she dances on a table. She's hot and a good dancer, but it still surprises him that people post videos like that for everybody to see. What if you were her boyfriend? How would you feel about guys sitting in their bedrooms watching her dance around in her underwear?

Mom's coming up the stairs, so he clicks out of YouTube.

"Liam." She knocks. "Can I come in?"

"Yeah."

"I am so proud." She rushes in and gives him a hug, which sends the chair spinning.

"Okay, Mom."

"That was a brave move and I admire you for it. Change doesn't happen when people sit back and wait. It comes from people with the courage to step forward and act. You did that and I'm proud of you."

"Dad wasn't pleased."

"Don't worry about that." She brushes her hair back. "He knows all those people at school and how they talk. Let them talk. They should be talking about this. A coach leading prayers at school — that's worthy of discussion."

Mom rambles on about constitutional principles, the Bill of Rights, and the intent of the Founding Fathers. She and Dad are completely different. Sometimes it would be nice if they were a little more alike. Sometimes it would be nice if she slowed down to ask him how he's doing.

"Are you ready to go?" She checks her watch.

"Where?"

"Church. The Romanos' presentation on their year at that orphanage in Mexico. I told you yesterday."

"I forgot."

"They're serving dinner. Tacos and quesadillas."

"I don't want to go." He slouches down in his chair.

"You like Mexican food. It will be fun. Anne said they've got terrific pictures of Chichen Itza."

"No, I've got homework. I'll stay here."

"Suit yourself. There's some meat loaf leftover in the fridge. We shouldn't be late." She looks around. "Liam, this room is a disaster. It wouldn't kill you to pick up a few things."

Liam spins around in his chair. A night alone sounds good. He can go back to watching that girl dance.

Dead Wrong

XXX Liam wakes to a massive headache on Thursday. He staggers from his bed to turn off the alarm and immediately goes back to lie down. The pain moves up steadily from the back of his neck and locks his head in a throbbing trap.

He doesn't want to go to school. He'd like to be someplace far away, like on a beach in Florida. Another gray day. It's been gray for an entire week now. Not a single glimpse of sun. Instead, a heavy cloud hangs over everything and doesn't move. He's had enough. It's like living in a cave.

He curls up in a ball under his duvet and feels the thumping of his headache. Dizzy scratches against the dresser, wanting him up. The headache isn't going away on its own. He needs some Advil to crack the pain.

On the counter he finds a note.

Liam,

I'm at a breakfast meeting downtown and Dad's at an All-Staff.

See you after practice.

Love, Mom

P.S. A ship in a harbor is safe, but that's not what ships are built for.

Dizzy meows like crazy, so he shakes food into her bowl. She snarfs it down quickly and meows strangely. She gags twice and pukes up on the floor. Disgusting. She bends down and starts to eat it. He pushes her away and wipes it up with paper towels. Chunky, warm, cat vomit. Nice way to start the day.

He washes his hands and looks in the mirror. Yikes. Bloodshot eyes squint back. He shakes out two Advil and downs them with water. He squeezes cream from the tube the dermatologist gave him and rubs it on the rash on his finger.

Back in his room, he checks his computer. Another e-mail from Mackenzie. Two in two days.

From: Mackenzie Kost
To: Liam Bergstrom

Date: February 10

Subject: sorry

liam,

hard to write so straight to the point. we should see other

people. sorry to break up by email but that's how its gotta

be. u didn't do anything wrong. please don't take this

personally. still friends?

lyl

kenz

What? He stares at the screen. The liar. Going out with

Jean-Baptiste behind his back.

He grabs the picture of her from his desk and slams it

to the floor. Glass shatters and he picks through the pieces to

pull the photo out. He rips her face. Again and again and

again until the pieces are so small, he can't rip anymore. He

walks to the bathroom and flushes the bits down the toilet.

Don't take it personally? He's the only other person affected

by her decision. Of course he takes it personally.

Still friends? No. Of course not. After this. Never.

He rereads the e-mail as if he'll find some new clue. He's been an idiot. She wasn't committed to him the way he was to her. He should be committed for being so stupid.

He holds his head in his hands and his headache pounds. He feels like he's shrinking.

He's never going to make the mistake of going out with anybody ever again.

XXX As soon as he walks into English, Mrs. Stabenow pulls him aside. "Principal Craney wants to see you immediately." She looks at him over the top of her glasses like she's trying to figure out why.

Liam feels a knot in his stomach as he walks past the trophy cases, the gold glory protected behind glass. Mackenzie's e-mail and now this. What a nightmare.

He checks in with Ms. Ayres, the secretary. "He's expecting you," she says grimly.

"What's the meaning of this?" Craney waves the letter as soon as he sees Liam.

"What?" Liam stands in front of the desk. Craney's a

huge guy with a buzz cut. He used to be the football coach. Liam's intimidated already.

"Don't play dumb with me." Craney points to one of two leather chairs. "Sit down."

Liam does as he's told and inhales the scent of fresh leather. Craney must have gotten new furniture.

"Were you the one who talked with this . . ." Craney peers at the letter. "Americans United for Separation of Church and State outfit?"

Liam considers denying it. How would Craney know? But he can't lie if he's angry with Coach for lying.

"Yes, sir," he says softly. He squeezes his hands so Craney won't see them shaking.

"The last thing we need is outsiders telling us how to run our school." Craney pounds his desk. "This group is from Washington, D.C. What do they know about Horizon? Do they understand how we do things here?"

Liam doesn't think he's supposed to respond, so he focuses on the goalpost lamp at the corner of Craney's desk and tries to hold still.

Craney looks at the letter and grimaces. "I'm going to be forced to conduct an investigation and interview people." He taps his finger on the paper. "Expect to be called back here next week."

"Yes, sir."

Craney sets his glasses on the desk and rubs his forehead. "Does your dad know about this?"

"Yes."

"I went to school with him and we played basketball together. He knows this isn't how we do things here." Craney points to the door. "Get out."

Bringing up Dad is a low blow. It wasn't his decision. He's not involved. Liam hurries down the hall, trying to get as far away from Craney as he can.

XXX After school, Liam walks into the locker room with his gym bag slung over his shoulder. He opens his locker and takes clothes off the hooks. He shoves his shoes, his socks, his ankle braces, and dirty jock in the bag. He throws in his shampoo, deodorant, comb, and cologne. He folds his jerseys and shorts neatly on the bench.

He looks around the room: all the sweat, the blood, the jammed fingers and twisted ankles. He takes his lock from the locker, clicks it closed, and tosses it in his bag.

He runs his hand across the top shelf of the locker. Nothing. He peels off the tape with his name, crumples it, and throws it in the trash. He takes one last look at the empty locker. He closes it, slings his bag over his shoulder, and grabs the folded shirts and shorts. He knocks on Coach's door.

"Come in."

"Coach, I'm sorry that I didn't tell you about the letter in advance."

"Sit down, Bergstrom," Coach says. "I've been expecting you."

Liam sets his bag down and sits in the metal chair.

"I'm disappointed. Very disappointed." Coach rubs his chin. "You let me down. You let the team down. Most importantly, you let yourself down."

Liam looks into Coach's blue-gray eyes and waits for more.

"The team is greater than the individual," Coach says.

"As a member of a team, it's necessary to focus on the good of the group. You didn't do that. You put yourself first. You thought you were better, more important. What you did was wrong, dead wrong."

"I don't see it that way." Liam stands and feels surprisingly clear. He doesn't have to listen to this. He sets the clothes on Coach's desk. "I quit."

Half-Closed Eye

XXX Liam gets in the car and drives. He doesn't know where he's going. He just drives. For the first time in years, he doesn't have practice or a game on a Thursday in February. For the first time in years, he's not on a team. He can do whatever he wants. But what?

He drives west past the turnoff to his house. He winds down the hill to the Kakabikans River and hits the brakes. Three deer stand still in the middle of the road. The buck has a ten-point rack that would make a fine trophy during hunting season. All three are bony with matted fur. It's been a hard winter — sharp cold and deep snow. Tough for them to find food.

The doe and the yearling bound up the hill to the west, while the buck crashes through brush below. Liam pulls the car to the shoulder and turns off the engine. He watches the spot where the buck disappeared behind the trees but nothing stirs.

He's off the team. So why doesn't he feel better?

When he talked to Megan, he was excited. But that's all evaporated.

Mackenzie and basketball — the two most important things in his life — are both gone. He takes off his glove and examines the white blister of the burn. It looks like a half-closed eye. Or half-opened, depending on how you look at it.

The river makes icy curves among the bare trees. Liam gets out and crunches snow as he steps downhill into the ravine. He follows the twists and turns of the ice, looking for signs of the buck. He picks up a smooth black stone that's lying on a stump. How did that get here? Maybe it washed up in a spring flood. He cleans sand off the stone and puts it in his pocket.

A flash of brown to his left makes him turn. The buck looks out from behind a clump of bushes twenty yards away. Liam stares back and tries not to move. He holds the buck's gaze and concentrates on not blinking. As large as the buck is, his eyes make him look vulnerable.

A grain truck roars by on the bridge and the spell is broken. The buck turns his head and bounds up the hill. Liam digs his boots into the snow to keep from slipping as he climbs back to the car.

He drives west past Dixon on the Old Fort Road and pulls into the empty parking lot of the wildlife management area. He zips his coat all the way up and ties his hood. It's windier out here than in the ravine. Mackenzie broke up with him four days before Valentine's Day. How romantic. At least now he doesn't have to buy her a stupid gift.

He trudges through knee-high snow to the frozen lake. Maybe quitting wasn't all that brave. Maybe part of it was fear. Maybe he was afraid of screwing up on varsity and this provided a way out.

He lies on his back and looks up at the gray sky. What's he going to do without basketball? What's he going to do without Mackenzie? He searches for a sign. Nothing. Just heavy clouds. He lies on snow that is on top of ice that is on top of water. Between the sky and the water, he is so small, so insignificant, so alone.

The ice groans as it shifts and his eyes moisten. He doesn't feel connected to anything. Tears roll down his face, and he does nothing to stop them as he lies on his back on the frozen lake.

XXX When Liam gets to his locker the next morning, Mr. Franzen, the art teacher, is waiting for him. He's tall and thin with a neatly trimmed goatee and rimless glasses.

"Good morning, Liam. I'm Jack. I coach the girls' basketball team. Do you have a minute?"

"Yeah." Liam matches his firm grip.

"I heard what happened with Principal Craney. How are you doing?"

"All right." Liam hangs his coat on its hook.

"I've got a proposal," Jack says. "We've got two weeks before regionals and I need a couple of guys to practice with the team. One of them needs to be a strong post player to bang around underneath. Would you be willing to join us?"

"Sorry, Coach. I'm not interested."

"No, no, not Coach." He holds up his hand. "Call me Jack."

"Okay." He can't say Jack. It's hard to call a coach anything other than Coach.

"Some of our younger players don't realize how good our opponents are going to be. They need a new challenge in practice."

"No thanks." Liam grabs his English book and stuffs it in his backpack.

"Please consider it." Jack holds out his palms. "I talked with Darius Buckner. He's joining us Monday. I'd love to have you there, too. You'd be a terrific addition."

"No, sorry."

Jack moves a step closer. "Principal Craney talked with all the coaches about the letter he received. I think what you did took courage. I think what you did was right."

"Thanks," Liam says softly. "I appreciate that."

"Consider joining us, Liam. It would be an honor to have you be part of our team."

Liam shakes his head. "Sorry. I'm not playing with girls."

XXX The night of the Sweethearts' Dance, Liam's shooting hoops at the Borton College Athletic Building because the Y is hosting a middle-school tournament. He can't stay away from the game. It's not about being on varsity. It's not about being the best sophomore post player. It's the game. He's pulled to the game like a magnet to metal.

He hits a jumper from the baseline, chases the ball down, then shoots from the other side. Back and forth, setting his feet even though he's exhausted. When he can't run anymore, he sees how many free throws he can make in a row.

Six.

Seven.

Too short.

One.

Two.

Three.

He was never going to this dance anyway because Mackenzie's in France. That was one of the good things about going out with her. He didn't have to worry about who to ask out. Now he's back to nothing.

He lines a bank shot off the board. He doesn't want to play with girls. The game would be slower, softer, boring. There would be less bumping and shoving. It would be a weak imitation of what he's missing.

He hears a ball bouncing at the other end and turns to see Darius release a three. Nothing but net. Darius jogs to the ball, dribbles behind the arc, and launches another. *Swish.*

Liam walks down. "Hey, what are you doing?"

"Shooting." Darius looks at him like he's asked a stupid question. "What are you doing?" He launches another jumper.

"Same thing. The Y has a tournament." Liam grabs the ball and passes to Darius, who makes another shot. "I heard you were going to practice with the girls' team."

"Yeah." Darius sets his feet and nails another three.

"Why?"

"Jack asked me and Leah's been begging me." Darius pump-fakes and lofts a fadeaway. "Are you going to do it?"

"I don't know." Liam rebounds the miss and dribbles along the baseline. He makes a fifteen footer and Darius passes him the ball. He steps back and makes another. Running with Darius might be fun. And pushing and holding with girls like Iris could be interesting. He shoots from deep in the corner and the ball hits the rim and bounces off. "I'm thinking about it."

Trails to Blaze

XXX Walking down the hall on Valentine's Day, Liam's assaulted by heart decorations. Red and pink shapes plaster the gray lockers and scream "I'm not a loser like you." Exactly what he needs — more reminders of his four-thousand-mile breakup.

"Quitter."

"Jerk."

"Atheist."

He overhears bits and pieces of conversation. It feels like everybody's talking about him.

In the back of the art room, Mr. Franzen is by himself. "Good morning, Liam." He tears off a chunk of clay.

"Morning."

"Buc, buc, buccaw." A giant chicken stumbles into the room. "Buc, buc, buccaw. Valentinegram."

Liam recognizes one of the guys from theater through the chicken's beak. How did he find him here? Did Mackenzie schedule this before breaking up with him?

"Roses are red, violets divine. But only you are my valentine." The chicken flaps his wings dramatically. "You are the grape to my wine. You are the eight to my nine. You will always be my valentine."

Mackenzie always went for that corny stuff. The chicken does a little dance and ends with an awkwardly landed split. "With love from your valentine, your wifey, Mrs. Jack."

"Bravo." Jack claps as the chicken bows and shakes his feathered butt in the air. Liam looks at the paint-stained floor. It didn't have anything to do with him. Jack presses the clay and turns on the pottery wheel. "Sorry," he says. "I need this for a demonstration piece. What can I do for you, Liam?"

"I've been thinking about your offer."

"Yes."

"What you asked about Friday." Liam rocks back and forth.

"Yes." Jack's hands move confidently even though he's not looking at them.

"I guess I'll do it."

"Excellent." Jack adds water with a sponge, and out of the muddy mess, a smooth edge emerges.

"There are three rules." Jack holds his hands steady as the wheel spins. "Number one, respect yourself. Number two, respect your teammates."

Those sound easy enough.

"Number three, no dating anybody on the team during the season. Can you handle that?"

"Yes, Coach. Sorry. I mean, yes, Jack."

Jack stops the wheel and inspects a finished bowl. "Practice is at three-thirty today in the main gym." He cuts the bowl from the clay and sets it on the board beside him. "You and Darius will dress in the gym locker room."

XXX "Principal Craney wants to see you again." Mrs. Stabenow raises her eyebrows as she writes out a pass. "You're getting to be a regular."

Liam trudges down the hall and stops at the art display case. Anything to delay talking to Craney. He spots the triangular tower and reads the card.

Darius Buckner
Sophomore
Title: Reaction

Liam gazes through the glass. What's it reacting to? Maybe Darius moving to Horizon. The face looks more fearful today. But maybe that's just him.

Liam resumes walking toward the office. Craney said he was going to interview people. Did he talk to Drake? Darius? Coach Kloss? Liam reaches into his pocket and squeezes the stone from the river he's been carrying around.

"Sit down, Bergstrom." Craney points to a chair when Liam walks in. "Let's make this quick. I've got lots of people to talk to."

Liam sits down in the leather chair as Craney opens a three-ring binder.

"Has Coach Kloss been leading Christian prayers in the locker room before boys' basketball games?" Craney leans over and squints at the paper.

"Yes." Liam nods.

"Has Coach Kloss been leading these prayers at halftime?"

"Yes."

"Does Coach Kloss encourage members of the basketball team to join in the prayers?"

"Yes." Liam uncrosses his legs. These questions are unbelievably easy.

"Does he encourage team members to lead these prayers?"

"Yes." Liam watches a cardinal peck at seed outside the window. Who put that feeder up? Craney doesn't seem like he'd be into birds.

Craney closes his binder and rubs his chin. "Tell me one thing, Bergstrom. What exactly is your objection to these prayers?"

Liam's stomach tightens. "Religion is kind of personal. Not everyone believes what Coach does." He leans forward. "Some people on the team feel left out. Some say things they don't believe to please Coach." He points to his chest. "That's what I did. It encourages hypocrisy." He pauses. "Anyway, it's unconstitutional for Coach to lead these prayers at school."

"Whoa," Craney says. "The lawyers will take care of that." He locks eyes with Liam. "You know you've opened up a can of worms, don't you?"

Liam shakes his head. "The can was open. It's been open a long time. I just told some people about it."

"That's enough, Bergstrom." Craney turns to watch the cardinal. "Back to class."

XXX Liam and Darius dress for practice in the beat-up gym locker room. Unlike the shiny benches of the basketball locker room, everything here is from the last century.

"Did Craney talk to you about Kloss?" Liam ties a double knot.

"No, why?"

"He got a letter about Coach leading prayers before games."

"What kind of letter?" Darius pulls up his shorts.

"A letter from a lawyer threatening to sue if Kloss doesn't stop." Liam kicks his locker to close it completely.

"Who contacted the lawyer?"

Liam taps his chest.

Darius's eyes widen. "No way! Quitting the team. Taking on Kloss. I didn't know you had it in you." He extends his fist and Liam pounds it.

"I told Craney you made me do it." Liam smiles.

"Get out of here." Darius gives him a shove and Liam slides away.

As they walk down the hall, Darius stretches his arms over his head. "I'm glad someone else is finally standing up to Kloss."

Liam stretches, too. Standing up to Kloss. Hearing Darius say it makes it sound stronger. "I've got another question."

"Yeah."

"Why is your sculpture titled *Reaction*? What's it reacting to?"

"Two things."

"What?"

"Life and death." Darius scrunches his eyebrows and tightens his mouth to look like the sculpture. "I practiced making faces in the mirror."

Liam laughs. He unwraps a piece of Trident. He's not sure

what to expect at practice, but with all those girls, he'd better have decent breath.

XXX Heads turn as Liam and Darius enter the gym. Leah Braverman, who's leading a stretching exercise with one leg bent behind her and the other in front, pauses. "Let's welcome Darius Buckner and Liam Bergstrom. They're going to practice with us for the rest of the year." Leah waves them forward. "Join the circle for Transition."

"Why do we need guys?" Jessica McAuliffe sits up. She's a junior and she's big. Not as tall as Liam, but she must weigh forty pounds more. She's got a tattoo of barbed wire around one arm and Scooby-Doo on the other.

Liam sits down next to Darius.

"It's girls' basketball." Chloe Keenan tightens the band on her ponytail. "It's only supposed to be girls."

"Yeah," Jessica says. "We're doing fine."

"Listen." Leah stretches to grab her foot. "Our goal isn't to do fine. Our goal is to win State. We won it my sophomore year and we had a couple of guys practice with us then. I want another championship, and to do that, we need to improve. We need Darius and Liam. It's not going to change the rotation in games. It's not going to change playing time. It's going to help us get better. Everybody got it?"

Liam looks over at Jack Franzen, who's sprawled out on the bleachers reading a book. He sure doesn't act like a coach.

"We don't need them," Jessica mumbles.

"Last stretch." Leah extends both legs in front of her and bends her head to her shins like she's made of rubber.

Liam tries to bend, but he can't even get halfway to his knees.

Leah sits up straight. "Who's got Game of the Day?"

"I do." Chloe raises her hand. "But now it doesn't seem right."

"What do you mean?"

"Well, I had a silly one for Valentine's Day, but I didn't expect we'd have guys." She glances at Liam and Darius.

"Jack talked with us last week about inviting them." Leah raises her voice.

"Yeah, but I didn't think they'd be crazy enough to say yes." A couple of girls laugh.

Liam looks down at the floor. He shouldn't be here if he's not wanted.

"Tell me the game." Leah slides over to Chloe, who whispers in her ear.

"That's okay," Leah says. "They're just guys."

"Maybe I should call it Duck, Duck, Goose," Chloe says.

"No." Leah shakes her head. "Keep it the way it is."

"Okay." Chloe rolls the sleeves of her shirt up. "The game is called Friends and Lovers. We need to move back and make this circle huge." She gestures for everyone to scoot back. "Three of you are going to be searchers who stand on the outside of the circle and run around tapping people's heads and saying 'friend' or 'lover.' If you get a friend tap, you stay sitting. If you get a lover tap, you chase that person around the circle and try to catch them before they can get back to your spot. If you catch the searcher, you get to go back to your spot."

"What if you don't catch them?" Leah asks.

"Then you stay a searcher," Chloe says. "You, Jess, and Iris will start out as searchers."

Liam sits cross-legged. What does this have to do with basketball? He feels like he's accidentally walked into a women's bathroom and can't get out.

"Friend." Iris taps him on the head.

"Friend." Jessica whaps him harder than necessary.

"Lover." Leah taps Darius, who jumps up for the chase. She races around the circle, but Darius closes fast.

He lunges for Leah right before she slides back into her spot. "I got you," he calls.

"Agghhh," she moans.

"Friend." Iris taps Liam again.

"Lover." Leah taps him on the head. He's watching Iris, so he's slow to jump up. Leah has a head start and dives into his spot before he can catch her. "You're a searcher, Liam."

"Friend, friend, friend." Liam runs around the circle, tapping heads. This game is silly. He's got to tap somebody who won't catch him.

"Lover." He taps Iris on the head. She's up quickly and chases after him. He runs hard past Jessica, who leans back to slow him down. Iris is right behind as Liam slides into place.

"You're a searcher again," he says, and she looks disappointed. Maybe he should have let her catch him. He watches everyone laughing and yelling. It's a way to run and make it less boring.

"Great game, Chloe," Leah says and the girls all stand. "Let's hear it for Chloe."

"Vada vim. Vada vom. Yom. Yom. Yom." The girls dance and shake. "Go, Chloe!" Liam looks to Darius, who shrugs. He doesn't have any idea what's going on either.

The rest of practice is a scrimmage. Liam, Darius, and three reserves run the offense and defense of Plainview, their next opponent, so the starters can get used to it.

"Don't let Leah have an open three, Darius." Jack stands on the edge of the court and is into practice now. "Make her put it on the floor. She likes to crossover and go left. Force her right."

Iris cuts underneath and Liam pursues. Jessica steps out, and Liam crashes into her. It's like running into a truck. She smirks above him as he's sprawled on the floor.

"You okay, Liam?" Jack asks.

"Yeah." He scrambles up. He didn't expect a screen like that from a girl. He scowls at Jessica, who flexes her muscles and grins.

Darius passes to Liam. The girls' ball is a little smaller than the one he's used to. He bounces it once and passes back to Darius, who hits a jumper.

At the other end, Liam guards Jessica. "Get up on your feet," Jack calls. "Have a lightness in your feet like you're about to lift off the ground."

Jessica calls for the ball and Leah passes it. "Don't let Jess go middle," Jack says. "Force her baseline, Liam." Jessica turns and Liam blocks her shot.

"Foul," she complains.

"Play through it," Jack says. "Jess, you'll be going against taller players in the playoffs. You can't go straight over the top of them the way you've done in conference. You need to make a move."

Jessica bumps Liam as he jumps for a rebound. If he doesn't play as hard as he can, he's going to get run over. These girls can play.

At the end of practice, players spread out and lie on their backs on the floor.

"Liam and Darius, join us," Jack says as he turns out the lights.

Everything is quiet in the dark and Liam hears Iris's breathing next to him.

"The river is never the same twice." Jack walks among them. "Your challenge is to be aware. Right here. Right now. Satisfaction comes from being deeply present in each moment."

Liam shifts his hips to get more comfortable. How can Jack see in the dark? What if he trips over someone?

"Horizon High School Blazers," Jack says. "Trailblazers. The word comes from scouts who rode ahead to make a mark, or a blaze, on a tree so others could follow. You each have trails to blaze." Jack stops walking and lets the words hang in the stillness. "You are Trailblazers."

Liam wiggles his ankle. How long do they have to lie like this?

"Tomorrow, Plainview visits," Jack says. "Don't make the game more complicated than it is. Basketball is beautiful in its simplicity." He pauses. "Visualize what you want to do on this court. Visualize how you will move. Visualize how you will feel with the ball in your hands."

Liam breathes in the smell of sweat and wood varnish. The only thing he can visualize is that his butt hurts.

Playing with Girls

XXX "Let's get this straight." Seth finds Liam at lunch. "You quit varsity basketball because of a few prayers."

"No. I quit because Coach lied to me. I didn't want to be on the team after that. And I'm sure Coach didn't want me to stay either."

"Duh. You got him in trouble by going behind his back." Seth sits down across from him. "And now you're playing with girls?"

"Yeah." Liam takes a gulp of chocolate milk. "In practice."

"You work your butt off to make varsity as a sophomore and then give it all up to play with girls." Seth shakes his head in disgust. "That's insane."

Liam dunks his grilled cheese in tomato soup. "I didn't expect you to agree, but you could pretend to try to understand."

Seth pulls at a candy wrapper that's stuck to his shoe. "Coach Kloss called me up to take your place."

"Congratulations." Liam tries to sound sincere.

"That isn't how it was supposed to be. We were supposed to be on varsity together." Seth looks up.

Suddenly Liam senses a presence behind him.

"Traitor," Pelke growls.

Liam feels a poke in the back and turns. Drake, Gund, and Pelke tower over him. "What?"

"Traitor." Gund pulls him up by the back of his sweater.

Seth starts to get up.

"Sit down, Crowley," Drake commands. "We'll take care of this."

Seth lowers himself back in his seat.

Pelke swings an elbow that cracks Liam's face. "I told you to leave it alone."

"Betrayer." Drake shoves him hard. Liam slams against the table, knocking over his tray and sending soup flying. Seth pulls back to avoid the mess.

"Don't bother to show up for work on Saturday." Drake pins Liam's arms behind his back. "You're terminated."

Gund puckers his lips and punches Liam in the gut.

Liam doubles over as his breath leaves his lungs. He grabs his stomach like he's trying to hold it in.

"Judas," Drake hisses from behind.

"Hey, what's going on over there?" Mr. Einerson, the lunchroom monitor, calls from the far side of the cafeteria.

"Nothing." Pelke holds up his hands.

"Break it up." Einerson starts over and the three of them scatter.

Liam touches his nose and blood covers his fingers. He grabs a napkin from the table and hurries to the bathroom.

The fight happened so fast; it was over before he threw a punch. Three against one — more like a mugging than a fight. And Seth didn't lift a finger to help. He did exactly what Drake told him. Screw him.

XXX That night the gym is packed, so Liam climbs the stairs to the balcony. With every breath, his ribs hurt. He can't find an open seat, so he stands in the corner listening to the crowd buzz with excitement. Where did all these people come from? There are twice as many fans as for a boys' game.

"When we say, 'Go,' you say, 'Blazers.'" The cheerleaders work the crowd. Liam didn't even know the girls had cheerleaders. "Go."

"Blazers!" the crowd yells.

"Go!"

"Blazers!"

"Go!"

"Blazers!" Feet stamp and it sounds like thunder. Plainview is second in the conference, but they don't look too confident now.

A roar erupts from the crowd as the Horizon players dressed in black warm-ups enter. They form two lines and their ponytails bob as they run down each side of the gym. Fans reach out to slap their hands as the band blasts out "Eye of the Tiger." The two lines pass under the basket, and players slap hands with one another and then circle back to midcourt.

They split into groups and run three offensive players

against two defensive ones. Chloe passes to Iris, who bounce-passes to Jessica. Jessica passes back to Chloe, who nails a jumper. Iris and Chloe switch to defense, and Iris blocks a reverse layup.

A guy with a rainbow-colored wig, Mardi Gras beads, and a tie-dyed cape shouts, "Let's go, Blazers."

Fans pick up the chant as drums pound out the four-syllable beat: "LET'S GO, BLAZERS!"

The Horizon players hold hands during the national anthem, and then the whole team gathers in a circle around Jack. The five starters peel off their warm-ups and make their own circle at center court with their arms around one another. Leah tells them something and they all laugh.

Liam watches Iris take her position at center court. Her short blond hair is tucked under a black headband and she looks sharp in her red-and-white uniform. The ref tosses the ball and Jessica tips to Leah. She spots an opening, drives to the hoop, and dishes to Iris, who gets fouled but still makes the basket. The crowd goes crazy.

"Way to go, Iris," a man in a John Deere hat yells.

Liam claps. That's exactly the way they practiced attacking the Plainview defense yesterday.

Iris misses her free throw, and Horizon hurries back on defense. They play a one-three-one zone that confuses Plainview. Iris slides strong to the corner and Liam stands on tiptoes to see.

Leah goes to the line and nails two free throws. She runs a nice game. She pushes the tempo but stays under control. She doesn't force passes but finds the right player, and when she drives into traffic, space always seems to open for her.

After a steal, Leah waits on the wing as Iris fights through a screen. Leah passes the ball to her, and she passes it back. Leah points to a spot to remind Iris to demand it. Iris gets the defender behind her and raises her hand to call for the ball. Leah delivers it.

Iris turns quickly to make the shot, and the crowd roars.

Jack stands and forms an X with his wrists. Horizon puts on the press. Chloe smothers the Plainview guard and steals the ball. She passes to Leah, who scores the layup. Plainview calls time-out with Horizon ahead eight to zero.

"Ashes to ashes. Dust to dust." Horizon cheerleaders lead the chant. "Sorry to beat you, but we must, we must." Liam's never heard this cheer. It's almost an apology. Sorry we're so good.

Horizon goes up by fourteen, and Jack substitutes freely. The Plainview players look like they don't know what hit them. The band hammers out the beat to "Another One Bites the Dust" and fans sing along.

At halftime Liam goes down behind the bench where Darius sits with the girls' JV players. "Hey."

"Where you been?"

"Upstairs. The place is jammed."

"Jack said to save a seat for you." Darius gestures to the spot next to him. "You okay?"

"Yeah." Darius must have heard about the fight. Liam sets his coat down. "What do you think so far?"

"Good start." Darius nods. "I've been thinking about practice. We've got to beat the starters tomorrow."

XXX After school Wednesday, Liam stares at his locker. Pieces of white athletic tape spell out:

He looks around to see if Drake or anyone else is following him. The halls feel much more threatening since the fight.

He peels at the tape — the same stuff they use to tape ankles in the basketball locker room. He steps back and studies the letters. He peels off the top *G* and sticks it beside the other one. He tears smaller pieces of tape from the *F* and the *A* and arranges them. He has just enough.

GOT GAME

It looks like a question, but it could also be an answer.

XXX At practice, Chloe leads the team in looking up at the ceiling for Transition. Liam lies on his back and adjusts his shoulders. "Imagine the ceiling is the floor and you have to walk on it," Chloe says. "Don't say anything and watch what comes into your mind."

Liam's ready to run, to burn off some frustration, to beat the first five — not lie here. How come everybody else seems so comfortable on the floor?

"Try to focus on one thing as a way to slow your mind," Chloe says softly.

He concentrates on the lights. What would it be like to walk among them? Would they be hot if you got near them? How about doors? If the ceiling were the floor, the doors wouldn't be at floor level. You'd have to climb up to get out.

Staring at the ceiling does feel relaxing in a strange way. Liam's mind drifts to the upcoming scrimmage, but he brings it back to the ceiling and moving around in a different plane. Then it locks in on Drake, Gund, and Pelke and what's next. It's difficult to bring it back from that.

"Who's got Game of the Day?" Chloe asks as she wraps her hair in a headband.

"I do." Leah raises her hand.

"What's it called?"

"Defend the First Amendment." She moves next to Liam.

He looks around. Is he supposed to know something about this?

"Liam felt something at school was wrong." She puts her hand on his shoulder. "He had a choice: Keep quiet or do something."

Liam looks down as everybody stares at him.

"I know his mom so I'm not surprised he took a stand." Leah turns to him. "Let's hear it for Liam for having guts."

"Vada vim. Vada vom. Yom. Yom. Yom. Go, Liam!" The girls and Darius cheer.

Liam smiles. "Thanks." The support of his teammates is huge.

Leah holds up two sheets of paper. "This is the First Amendment." She bends down to lay one on the floor. "A copy will be set deep in each team's territory. The goal is to bring it back, but if you get caught, you'll go to prison. You can't get out until a teammate rescues you."

"Like Capture the Flag," Chloe says.

"No." Leah shakes her head. "Like Defend the First Amendment." She takes the second copy to the other end and splits everybody up into teams. "Go," she hollers.

Liam races down the side.

"Nobody's touching this," Jessica growls.

Iris sneaks up on Liam and tags his back. "Come with me." She leads him to the corner.

He squirms to shake loose, but Iris wraps both arms around him tightly. Being squeezed by her feels kind of good.

"Help," he shouts. He doesn't want to stand here while

everybody else is running around. Finally Chloe sees an opening and rushes to tag him before Darius can catch her.

"Thanks, Chloe." He holds her hand as she leads him back to their territory.

"No problem, Jail Boy." She laughs.

Everyone runs around the floor and goes in and out of prison, but neither team can get to the First Amendment.

"I'll run at Jessica," Liam whispers to Chloe and Leah. "Then you race in from opposite sides. Iris can't tag you both."

"Good plan." Chloe runs to one side and Leah the other.

Liam darts in and avoids Darius. He comes up behind Jessica. "Give me the First Amendment."

"Dream on." Jessica lunges for him.

He jumps out of reach and slides to the floor. Iris rushes to tag him. "More prison time for you."

Jessica stabs at Leah, but Chloe grabs the Constitution and races back. "I've got it. I've got the First Amendment." She jumps up and down.

Jack gets up and sets his book down. "Starting five in red. We'll play first team to thirty."

Iris takes off her white jersey and turns it inside out to the red side. She's wearing a tight T-shirt underneath that says HOOPS DIVA. Liam watches her slide the red side over her head. She's got a nice body. Then he remembers Jack's rule about respecting his teammates. It's not disrespect if he's respecting her body.

The scrimmage is intense. Darius keeps taking the ball hard to the hoop. It's obvious how much he wants to beat the girls today.

"Overplay his right hand, Leah," Jack directs. "Force him left. Keep him out of the lane."

Liam squeezes past Jessica for a rebound.

"Keep in front of him, Jess," Jack calls. "Box out. You've got to keep a body on a good rebounder."

Liam passes out to Nikki Martin, a red-haired senior who's Chloe's backup. She passes to Darius, who gets double-teamed by Leah and Jessica but still forces up a shot.

"Darius, if you're doubled, someone else is open," Jack says. "Trust your teammates."

Nikki passes back to Liam, who hesitates.

"Take it to the hoop," Darius says.

Liam bounces the ball tentatively and Jessica slaps it from his hands. Leah grabs the ball and leads the break the other way.

"Do something with the ball," Darius says. "Make a move."

Liam turns away. He's playing hesitantly, trying to avoid a mistake, rather than making something happen. He holds his elbow against Iris's back on a switch. She pushes back, and he breathes in a mix of her sweat and perfume. It's surprisingly sexy.

"Trust yourself, Iris," Jack says. "Demand the ball. This game is not complicated. You have to want the ball, and when you get it, if someone else is open, pass it to her."

Liam slides around Iris to deny the entry pass. Her game is a lot like his. What Jack is telling her applies to him, too.

The action is fierce and by the end, Liam's dragging to get

up and down the court. The game is close, but the starters win on Chloe's three-pointer.

Darius slams the ball down. "C'mon, Liam. We need more from you."

Liam kicks the ball across the gym. He needs to do more. He needs to trust himself. Like Jack says, he needs to demand the ball.

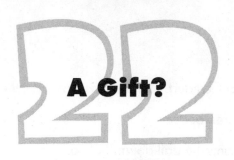

A Gift?

XXX "Love is not easy." Father Connell's deep voice carries through the church as he delivers his homily. "We are called to love one another. We are called to love those who are different from us. And because we are human, that is difficult."

Liam flashes back to Mackenzie. She was different and he loved her.

"We must love others for who they are, not for who we want them to be."

He loved being with her and holding her, but did he really love her? Maybe he loved the idea of having a hot girlfriend more than he actually loved *her*?

"Love is not something we do once and are set," Father Connell says. "Love is an ongoing struggle to reach for our higher selves, to follow the example of Jesus Christ and to treat others in his image."

Liam rubs his thumb against the palm of his left hand as light streams through the stained glass. Love is difficult. He loves his parents, but he doesn't always show them that.

They love him, but it doesn't always feel like that when Dad's disappointed or Mom's telling him what to do. The easiest person to love is Grandma. She loves him the way he is. Except on the days she forgets who he is.

"Lord, we pray to you," Father Connell says. "Help us to follow Your commandment to love one another. Help us to follow Your example and give us strength as we move forward in love and humility."

XXX After church, Liam sits across from Mom and Dad at Connie's Cafe, their Sunday favorite. "How's practicing with the girls' team?" Mom stirs Sweet'N Low into her cup.

"Different."

"In what way?" Mom sips and frowns.

"Jack's different. He's the coach, Jack Franzen. He reads books during Transition and Game of the Day and lets the girls lead them."

"I wonder how long he'd last if they didn't win conference every year," Dad says.

"Excuse me." Mom waves the waitress over. "I hate to complain, but this coffee's cold."

"I'm sorry." The waitress picks it up. "I'll bring you a new one. What about you, sir?"

"No, mine's fine." Dad catches Liam's eye. He never sends anything back. If he ordered chicken and the waitress brought him a hamburger, he'd eat it and think he should have ordered that in the first place.

Mom sees the look. "I can't help it if I like my coffee hot. Coffee is supposed to be hot."

"What do *you* do at the girls' practice?" Dad asks.

"Everything. Well, not everything. Darius and I dress in a separate looker room. But we do Transition and Game of the Day and then we scrimmage. We run some of the upcoming opponents' plays and their defenses to help the starters prepare."

"Do you miss boys' varsity?" Dad asks.

"No."

"Not at all?" Dad looks surprised.

"No. I've moved on." Liam twists his napkin. Dad must have had to explain to his friends why his son quit varsity. That must have been hard.

"I understand." Dad looks down. "I thought you still might miss it."

Liam hates it when Dad's right. Of course he misses the boys' team, but he can't admit that to Dad. The waitress brings their food and Liam drenches his buckwheat pancakes in blueberry syrup. The weight of Dad's disappointment hangs in the silence.

"Your dad thinks once you join a team, you have to finish." Mom sips her coffee. "Isn't that right, honey?"

Dad cuts his waffle. "Yes, usually."

"I couldn't do that, Dad."

"I'm sure that's true."

Liam chews a mouthful of pancake. It sounds like Dad's the one who really misses him being on varsity.

XXX Monday afternoon, the wind bites as Liam hikes across the parking lot. He ducks his head and covers his face with a glove. When's it ever going to warm up?

Inside the car, he turns the key and shifts into drive. *Falump. Falump.* Sounds like he's run over a piece of metal.

Falump. He pulls over and checks the tires. The driver's side looks fine, but the front passenger-side tire is totally flat. What lousy timing.

He hauls the jack and the spare from the trunk. The metal jack is freezing. He sets it in place and pumps the handle. He pushes on the tire iron, but the lug nuts won't budge. It's probably been a long time since they've been off, and the cold makes everything harder. He scans the parking lot for help, but nobody is around. There's a can of WD-40 in the emergency kit in the trunk. He shakes the can and sprays it on the lug nuts. He grabs the tire iron and presses with all his strength. Nothing.

He sprays more WD-40 and gives it time to soak in. He jumps from one foot to the other, trying to stay warm as the sun drops down behind a cloud. What a pain.

When he leans on the tire iron again, the nut slowly shifts, and he pushes with all his strength. He repeats the steps with the other three nuts and then removes the flat. He grabs the spare, lifts it on, and tightens it in place.

J & S Auto is still open, so he pulls in and shows the flat to

Steve, the mechanic. "Can you fix this? I must have picked up a nail."

Steve rolls the tire around and finds a half-inch gash. "You see this? That's no nail. That's a knife slash. Any idea who'd do that to you? Is someone out to get you?"

"Yeah," Liam says. "But don't say anything about it to my dad."

XXX When Liam walks onto the floor for practice, something's different. People are speaking softly and Iris has her arm around Chloe, who's wiping away tears.

Liam grabs a ball from the metal cage and dribbles down to Darius. "What's up?"

"Chloe broke up with Pelke." Darius shoots an off-balance jumper. "She caught him making out with Trisha Norwood by the pool. She's taking it hard."

Liam banks a shot in off the glass. Taking it hard. How else can you take it?

"He's a jerk," Jessica says to Chloe. "You're better off without him. You deserve somebody decent."

Chloe's still crying, so Jessica flexes her biceps to make her Scooby tattoo talk. "Ruh-roh. Bad behavior by Pelke. Rokay. Time to move on." It's a good Scooby voice and Chloe laughs through her tears.

Liam's shot bounces hard off the rim and rolls down toward Chloe. He chases after it and detours over to her. "Sorry, Chloe."

"Yeah." She tries to smile.

"As bad as it feels, it will get easier." He sounds like Dr. Phil. "Keep putting one foot in front of the other."

"Thanks, Liam." She dries her eyes on the sleeve of her jersey.

At the next hoop Leah and Iris are warming up. "How's Shea doing?" Leah bounces two balls at the same time.

"Still struggling." Iris misses a left-handed layup.

Liam turns to Chloe. "Who's Shea?" Maybe talking about someone else will help.

"Shea Donnelly. She started on varsity last year." Chloe rubs her nose and sniffles. "She's a great post player, and she and Iris are close." Chloe tosses a shot from the lane and Liam rebounds. "Her dad got this super important job with FedEx and they moved to Memphis over the summer. Shea hates it there. We all wish she was back here, especially Iris." Chloe shoots from the side. "As well as we're playing, we'd be better with Shea."

"Wow." Liam rebounds the miss. "It's hard to imagine this team being even better."

XXX At the end of practice, everybody shoots free throws, and Liam partners with Iris. He bounces the ball and positions his feet. He likes this smaller ball. It makes his hands feel bigger, makes him feel bigger. His shot rolls in to make him fourteen of twenty, and he switches places with Iris.

"What's yours, Darius?" Jessica is going around asking everybody's middle name.

"James." He swishes his shot.

"What about you, Iris?"

"Marie." Her shot rims out. "My grandma's name."

"How about you, Liam?"

"I'd rather not say."

"What?" Jessica looks surprised.

"It's a family name on my dad's side." Liam rebounds another miss by Iris.

"Well, lots of these are family names," Jessica says.

"Tell us." Chloe joins in. "Now we're curious."

"Pass."

"How bad can it be?" Darius asks.

"Bad." Liam chases down another miss.

"Iris, let's try something." Jack steps in and holds out his hands. "Sometimes it's helpful to mix things up."

She passes the ball to him.

"You don't have to shoot from here." Jack stands at the line straight out from the hoop. "Everybody does because it's the shortest distance. But you can actually shoot from any-where in the circle behind the line."

Jack fires from two feet behind the line and makes it. He's got a smooth shot. Liam rebounds the ball and throws it back. Jack moves over to the right side of the line and bounces the ball. "I played with a guy in college who shot his free throws from here. He didn't feel comfortable straight on, so he switched to the side and became a better free throw shooter. Try it."

Iris goes to the right side, just inside where the line meets the circle. Her shot goes in. Liam passes the ball back. Her second shot hits the front of the rim, bounces up, and falls off. "That would have gone in if I was shooting straight on," she says.

"Maybe," Jack says, "but you're shooting from this spot now. Relax into it and make the shot."

Iris aims and hits her third shot. "I kind of like it."

"Shoot from here for a while and see what happens." Jack moves to the next hoop to talk with Chloe. He says something and she laughs.

Iris swishes another one. "It's strange. I do feel more comfortable here." She passes the ball to Liam. "Try it."

He goes to the side. It's like shooting from Thailand in Around the World. That's always been one of his best shots. He makes the first one. "I like it, too," he says. "I didn't know you could shoot from here."

"Me neither." Iris passes the ball. "That's why Jack's the coach."

When everybody finishes free throws, Jack carries out a cardboard box. "At the start of the year, you got prose," he says. "For the playoffs, you get poetry." He reads out names and passes out books.

Liam looks around. Poetry at basketball practice? What's next? Knitting? Sharing feelings in a circle? Why aren't people complaining? He tries to catch Darius's eye, but he's talking to Leah.

"Liam." Jack gives him a book, and Liam studies the Post-it note.

Inscriptions - One's Self I Sing, page 5
Song of Myself - pages 25 to 68

"These books are for you to keep," Jack says. "Read them. Write in them. Think about them. I want you to memorize a poem, a section of a poem, or some lines that mean something to you. I'll meet with each of you in two weeks to talk about it."

Liam studies the green cover. *Leaves of Grass* by Walt Whitman. Homework at basketball practice. Whoever heard of that? He walks over to Darius, who's paging through his book. "What did you get?"

"*American Sublime* by Elizabeth Alexander," Darius says. "I've never heard of it."

"I've never heard of *Leaves of Grass*." Liam opens the book to a picture of a man with a long white beard. Why did Jack choose this book for him? It's like unwrapping a gift from your parents and not knowing if it's something you want or something they think you need.

Make a Move

XXX Since he's not working at Shoe Source on Saturdays anymore, Liam swings by the nursing home. He doesn't miss working with Drake and Pelke, but he got fired before he got to use his discount. He didn't even get new shoes out of the deal. He knocks gently on Grandma's door in case she's taking her afternoon nap.

"Yes," she says weakly.

"It's me. Liam." He walks to the chair where Grandma sits in the sunlight.

"Liam." Grandma stares at him. Her straight gray hair is pulled back neatly and she's wearing her dark blue dress with the yellow flowers.

"Here are some cookies Mom made." He holds out the tin.

"Liam," she says again.

He opens the lid and lets her see them. "Rosettes, your favorite."

"Loverly." Grandma picks one out. "Help yourself."

Liam lifts a butterfly-shaped cookie and takes a bite. A piece crumbles and he catches it against his shirt.

Grandma slowly takes a nibble. "*Mmmm.*"

Liam sits down in the recliner and watches Grandma take tiny bites. Father Connell talks about love and humility. That's Grandma. She's never had loads of money, but she always contributes to Habitat for Humanity and famine relief. She helps out when people are in trouble and never calls attention to it. That's the way she lives her life.

They sit in silence for a while. Grandma seems more alert today. Sometimes she doesn't remember things from the present well, but she's clearer about the past, like when she was young. "Grandma, what was school like when you were a girl?"

"Oh, that's so long ago." She looks like she's surprised. "I didn't speak English, only Swedish."

Liam leans forward to hear her raspy voice. "I know."

"My first day I sat next to Anna Norby." Grandma speaks slowly. "The teacher said something and Anna and the other students laughed. When I got home I told my mother that I sat next to Anna and everything was in English." Grandma sets her cookie down. "My mother asked if Anna could speak

English. I said, 'I don't know, but she can laugh in English.' I meant she understood the joke, but my mother thought what I said was so funny."

Liam licks sugar off his fingers. He's so glad Grandma is still able to tell one of her stories.

"Your dad was here this morning. He said you took a stand against your coach." Grandma takes a sip of water.

Liam wipes his hands on his jeans. Megan said she'd let him know Craney's response. What's taking so long?

"Your dad said he was proud."

Liam looks up. Proud? Dad didn't tell him that.

"Good for you." Grandma holds out her wrinkled hand.

Liam squeezes it gently. "Thanks, Grams."

XXX At the regional final, Horizon's up by fifteen. Jessica's dominating inside. Leah's making good decisions, and Iris is demanding the ball on the block and making strong moves.

Jack sits on the bench with his hands folded and legs crossed. Compared to most coaches, he doesn't say much during games. He lets the players play. He doesn't even call many time-outs. He lets the players figure it out and work through it.

Liam leans over to Darius. "They look good."

"It's going to get tougher. We have to beat them in practice to get them ready."

"I was thinking the same thing," Liam says, though he wasn't. He was thinking how smoothly Iris moves and how great she looks. She anticipates a pass and reaches for a steal. "You're in art with Iris, aren't you?" He tries to sound casual.

"Yeah."

"How well do you know her?"

"Some. She's kind of shy."

"I know." Liam clears his throat. "Does she have a boyfriend?"

"Iris?"

"Yeah."

"No." Darius shakes his head. "No boyfriend."

Liam watches her grab another rebound and pass to

Leah. No boyfriend — just what he was hoping to hear. Leah makes a smooth move and goes in for a layup. Liam and Darius stand and clap.

"Where's Leah going to school next year?"

"Princeton, Columbia, or Brown," Darius says. "Her mom wants Princeton. Her dad wants Columbia. Leah likes Brown. Bet on Brown."

Liam watches her sprint back on defense. Those are the types of choices Mom dreams about. She'd give anything for a kid like that. He scans the crowded arena and remembers the half-filled gym of the boys' games. He turns to Darius. "Do you ever miss playing with the guys?"

"What guys?"

"The boys' varsity."

"Nah. That wasn't real basketball. I play pickup over at the B-CAB. Two of the guys are out of town for a wedding this weekend. We could use another body. Can you play tomorrow at noon?"

"Sure." College guys will be a step up, but after sitting and watching tonight, he's ready for some action.

"So if you're going to run with us, I need to know one thing," Darius says.

"Yeah?"

"What's your middle name anyway?"

Liam rubs his forehead. "Norbert."

"You're right," Darius says. "That's bad."

XXX When Liam arrives at the gym, seven players are pushing under the hoop in an intense game of twenty-one. He checks them out as he puts on his shoes. Darius and two other black guys and four white guys. Most of them are built like football players.

Liam ties his shoes tightly. Darius should come over, but he's focused on the game. Liam walks slowly across the empty floor toward the hoop.

"Six." Darius shoots from the arc and makes it. "Seven." He makes it again. "Eight." He finally sees Liam. "Hey, everybody, this is Liam. He's going to run with us today."

"Hey," a few guys say.

Liam moves to the free throw line. Twenty-one has never

been his game because it's everybody against the guy with the ball. You need to have good moves to get a shot off.

"Darius is high with eight," a guy with a full beard says. "Straight up."

Darius drives baseline and gets smacked on the head. He doesn't call a foul or complain, but jumps out on defense on the guy who hit him. He slaps at the ball and it bounces to Liam. Straight up means he can go right up with it, but two defenders close fast, and he's afraid they'll block his shot. He dribbles the ball to the arc and hesitates.

A short white guy jumps out. "Let's see what you got."

Liam crosses over on his dribble, but the guy strips him cleanly. Liam retreats under the basket. Players muscle for position, yank rebounds, and slap the ball away from each other. Liam doesn't have a single point by the time Darius hits twelve.

"Thirteen," Darius calls as his shot falls through. Liam positions himself to the left of the basket. He needs to be more aggressive. Darius's shot bounces up and hits the rim twice. Liam times his jump and grabs the rebound. He turns to shoot a fadeaway and the ball banks in off the board.

"Nice hoop," Darius calls.

Liam moves to the top of the key. This is the other reason he doesn't like twenty-one. Everybody watches while you shoot. He bounces the ball once and launches it. The ball hits the front of the rim and falls short.

Three guys crash together and one taps the ball out. Darius seizes it and goes up for a shot. A guy hits him hard on the wrist. "That's what happens when you have the lead."

An older black man with dreads gives Darius a shove. Darius laughs and pushes back. Liam grabs another rebound and forces up an awkward runner that's not even close.

Darius fakes two guys off their feet and hits a jumper for twenty-one. As winner, he picks first for teams. He takes Liam second, and Liam's relieved not to be picked last.

"Liam, this is Cadillac." Darius stands next to the older guy with dreads. "Feed him the ball and good things will happen."

"I'm Sully." A white guy with a mustache slaps Liam's hand.

"If you pass it to Sully, you won't get it back." Darius dribbles over to him.

"Same with Arius." Sully steals the ball from Darius. "Arius because there's no D in his game. He's always looking to shoot."

Perfect. With three shooters, Liam can concentrate on defense and rebounding. He passes to Cadillac to start the game. Cadillac turns and shoots. One–nothing. This is going to be easy.

Liam guards his guy. He's a few inches shorter but built like a tank. Liam boxes him out, and Cadillac grabs the rebound and finds Sully.

Sully streaks downcourt and looks for his shot. He's cut off, so he passes to Darius, who finds Liam in the post. Liam passes to Sully, who shoots and misses.

"Go at your guy," Darius says. "You've got a height advantage. Shoot over the top of him."

Next time down, Darius passes to Liam again. Why doesn't Darius feed Cadillac like he said? Liam's defender elbows him in the back, and Liam looks to pass it back to Darius. He hesitates and the ball is knocked loose.

"C'mon, Liam. Make a move!" Darius shouts.

Liam posts up underneath. Darius wants him to improve his offense, but he doesn't need to point it out in front of everybody.

"Foul," Sully calls on a drive.

"What?" The guy with the beard gets in his face. "No blood. No foul."

"My call," Sully shoots back.

"That's weak, man. You lost the ball on the way up."

Liam waits for somebody to break up the argument, but nobody does.

"Show some game," Beard Guy challenges.

"Give me the ball." Sully pushes past his guy and goes right at Beard Guy.

"You got nothing," Beard Guy says.

"Yeah? Stop this." Sully jab-steps, then moves back for a three.

Beard Guy leaps and gets a piece of the shot. "Nothing," he hollers.

Darius grabs the loose ball and fires a pass to Liam. "Go at him."

✖✖✖ After school on Monday, Liam spots Drake walking to his Mustang. For once he's by himself, not with his pack. Liam jumps over puddles from the melting snow as he jogs to catch up with him. "Drake."

Drake whirls around. "What do you want?"

"You." Liam points.

"What do you mean?"

"If you've got a problem with me, be a man." Liam squints into the sun. "Don't slash my tire or send somebody else to do it."

Drake clicks open his trunk.

"Talk to me, Drake."

"I'll talk to you when I want to."

"Then talk." Liam moves to avoid the sun and crosses his arms like he's not budging.

"You ruined our season, Bergstrom."

"What are you talking about?"

"You wrecked our team spirit."

"C'mon, Drake. Good teams don't go on about team

spirit. They have it. You're just looking for somebody to blame."

"I am not."

"You're the captain."

Drake grabs a box of Adidas from the trunk. "By the way, Bergstrom, I'm leading prayers now. They're voluntary, but we've got plenty of volunteers."

Go at Her

XXX Liam rubs his forehead. Basketball homework. How did he get stuck with such a difficult book?

> *Of Life immense in passion, pulse, and power,*
> *Cheerful, for freest action form'd under*
>   *the laws divine,*
> *The Modern Man I sing.*

And why is this guy singing about everything?

> *All goes onward and outward, nothing collapses,*
> *And to die is different from what any one*
>   *supposed, and luckier.*

Liam thinks about this. Death might be different from what anyone supposed, but luckier? Grams says she's had a full life and that she's grateful for everything. She's less afraid of death than anyone he knows. Would she consider death luckier than being alive, though?

He struggles with long lists of people and places. He turns to the glossary to look up words he doesn't understand. He's supposed to be finished with this by next week, so he reads on about boatmen, clam diggers, and runaway slaves. How will he ever memorize any of this? He needs a break, so he checks his e-mail.

From: Mackenzie Kost

To: Liam Bergstrom

Date: March 7

Subject: miss you!

liam,

I bet u are surprised to get this after what happened but i miss u. jeanbaptiste is a jerk. i should have known better. >:-<

i am fed up with france and wish i was home.

i am really sorry. whats up with u?

lyl

kenz

x o x o x o

Liam rereads the message. Sounds like she got dumped. Too bad. He hits DELETE and the message disappears from his screen.

XXX "Stand in one place and imagine you are a tree." Iris leads Transition. "Put your hands above your head and move them in a gentle breeze." Liam raises his arms. "The wind blows stronger now and moves the trunk." She sways her hips. He moves his hips and tries not to stare too hard at Iris's. "Huge storm now." She swings back and forth. "The tree bends, but does not break." Everybody shakes all over and Liam smiles at being among all these willowy trees in the storm.

"The wind dies down and the tree stands tall," Iris declares. The players freeze in place with outstretched arms. Iris slowly lowers her hands to her sides and everybody follows.

"Thanks, Iris," Leah says. "Chloe, you've got Game of the Day?"

"Shoot. I forgot," Chloe says.

"Anybody else got a game?"

"I do." Liam steps forward.

"What's it called?"

"Banking Around the World."

"What are we going to do?" Jessica asks. "Exchange money?"

"You all know how to play Around the World." Liam grabs a ball. "Start here." He banks a layup off the board. "Then you go to all the other spots. But you have to bank your shot. If you make it without hitting the board, you have to start all over. Also, you have to pick a different country name for each spot. Run down all your misses."

Everyone spreads out at different hoops.

"One, two, three, go," Liam shouts, and balls fly. Players make their layups and move to the second spot. Most make their second shot and move to the corner of the free throw line.

"Oh, no." Iris swishes her shot and has to start over. "I finally get that shot down and now I have to bank it."

"Yes." Darius banks his in. "Argentina."

Players chase down rebounds and launch shots. Country names alternate with cries of frustration as players make shots and miss. Everybody is struggling, with one exception.

Liam watches Jessica, who's quietly progressing. She uses the board a lot in her game, so maybe she's used to looking for it. She banks a shot from Iris's free throw spot, chases the ball, and lines up her next one. She's almost finished.

Chloe swishes another free throw. "No." She jumps up and down and her ponytail flaps like a flag.

"I'm done!" Jessica hollers.

"No fair," Chloe says. "I'm back at the beginning."

Liam goes over to Jessica. "What were your countries?"

"United States, China, Iraq." Jessica pauses. "Finland, Sweden, Denmark, Norway, Iceland."

"Banking around the world in record time, Jessica is the champion." He holds up her arm like a boxer's.

"Good Game of the Day." Jessica slaps his hand. "Let's hear it for Liam."

"Vada vim. Vada vom. Yom. Yom. Yom." Everybody dances and shakes arms. "Go, Liam!"

"Scrimmage time." Jack walks onto the court. "Starters in red today."

Iris pulls off her jersey, showing a black sports bra underneath. Liam watches her turn the jersey inside out to red. She glares at him and he looks away.

"Let's have a good run." Jack claps.

Liam pushes Jessica under the hoop, and she elbows him in the head. Darius passes the ball to Liam and he sends it back.

"Go at her." Darius passes the ball back in.

Liam turns and shoots over Jessica.

"That's there, Norbert," Darius says. "Take it."

"Norbert. Is that your middle name?" Jessica laughs.

Up and down they go. Liam's more confident on offense after making that first hoop. He can shoot over Jessica. He calls for the ball and scores again.

"Jess, that's too easy," Jack says. "Move him off his spot. Make him work harder."

Chloe doubles down on Liam, but he sees Nikki open at the arc. He passes to her and she buries the three.

"Chloe, stay with the shooter," Jack says. "You can't leave her open."

The game is fast and intense. Jessica banks in two shots in a row.

"You've got to get out on her, Liam," Jack says.

With the game tied, the starters work the ball for the winning shot. Leah passes to Chloe, who dumps it into Jessica. Liam pushes against Jessica to keep her out of the paint. She passes to Iris, who swings it to Chloe at the top of the key.

Darius flies out and tips the shot. Liam snags the rebound and passes to Darius, who dribbles upcourt. One shot to win.

Darius passes to Liam, who passes it right back. The game's on the line, and he's not taking any chances. Darius will hit the game winner. Chloe jumps out to double team, and Darius passes back to Liam. Liam makes a tentative move baseline, looks to Darius, and then passes back.

Leah dives in for the steal. She hurries downcourt and finds Chloe in the corner. Darius is all over her, so she passes to Jessica, who turns and banks it off the board for the win.

"Banking Around the World," she hollers. Leah and Iris rush up to her and Chloe jumps up and down.

Liam looks to Darius, who shakes his head. "My bad." He pats his chest. "I blew it."

"You did," Darius shouts. "You need to go to the hoop."

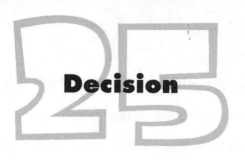

Decision

XXX "Let's talk about *Leaves of Grass*." Jack sits next to Liam on the bleachers while the rest of the team shoots free throws.

"It was hard at first," Liam says. "The old-fashioned language was confusing, and I didn't get what it was supposed to symbol —"

"Looking for symbols is one of the worst things to do with poetry," Jack interrupts. "Start with the language, the sounds, how the words go together, what you like about it."

Liam stretches out his legs. "I like Whitman's lists of the different people he feels connected to. He feels connected to everybody, everything, including animals and nature."

"Yes." Jack smiles.

Liam flips to a passage he's highlighted and reads:

> *I hear bravuras of birds, bustle of growing wheat,*
> *gossip of flames, clack of sticks cooking my meals,*

I hear the sound I love, the sound of the human voice,
I hear all sounds running together, combined, fused
  or following,
Sounds of the city and sounds out of the city, sounds
  of the day and night.

"Beautiful," Jack says.

"I also like it when he talks about animals." Liam finds
that section and reads:

I think I could turn and live with animals, they're so
  placid and self-contain'd,
I stand and look at them long and long.
They do not sweat and whine about their condition.

"True," Jack says. "What lines did you memorize?"
Liam shuts his book and begins:

But each man and each woman of you I lead upon
  a knoll,
My left hand hooking you round the waist,

My right hand pointing to landscapes of continents
and the public road.
Not I, not any one else can travel that road for you,
You must travel it for yourself.

"Exactly." Jack beams. "That's Whitman. It's your road, Liam."

Liam nods as balls echo and shoes squeak. Whitman pays attention to everything. What would he notice here? The colors of the jerseys, the sounds of the balls going through the nets, the connectedness of everyone on the team working together.

"Liam, this is for you." Jack reaches into a cloth bag and takes out a wooden box.

Liam lifts the lid and pushes aside newspaper. He uncovers a ceramic bowl with a gray-green glaze. The smooth shape looks like the shell of a turtle. "Wow."

"It's a celadon bowl, the piece I was making when you agreed to be on the team."

"It's beautiful." Liam turns the bowl over. "Thanks, Jack."

"Thank you, Liam, for saying yes." He holds out his hand and Liam shakes it.

Liam sets the bowl gently in the box and places it underneath the bleachers to protect it. He walks back onto the court to join his teammates. *My road. Not Mom's. Not Dad's. Not Mackenzie's. Not Jack's. Not Whitman's. My road.*

XXX "What do you got, Old Man?" Darius challenges Sully as he bounces the ball between his legs at the B-CAB.

"I'll shut you down." Sully crowds close.

Darius jab-steps, fakes a jumper, and drives to the hoop. Sully chases after and pushes Darius as the shot rolls off.

Liam grabs the rebound and goes right back up. Cadillac hits him on the shoulder, but Liam plays through it. You don't call a foul in this game.

Darius's hook shot rolls off, and Liam slides past Cadillac for the rebound. He fakes and gets Cadillac in the air before spinning the other way.

"Strong move, Norbert."

Liam grabs the ball. There's no way he's going to get Darius to stop using his middle name. "Eleven." He shoots from the arc. "Twelve." He's been practicing shooting just for this. "Thirteen." He misses the next one and Darius picks up the long rebound. Liam hops out to defend him.

"Let's go." Darius bounces the ball and then goes up for a shot. Liam leaps for the fake, and Darius ducks under and banks it off the board.

"Banking Around the World, Norbert." He raises his arms.

In the game, Darius feeds Liam inside. Liam makes a move to the hoop and is double-teamed, so he kicks a pass back to Darius, who drains it. Making a move opens space for Darius to score. The game isn't that complicated.

XXX Liam rushes to his locker after school Friday. No teachers for two days. On his phone, there's a missed call from area code 202. Where's that? He returns the call.

"Hello, Americans United for Separation of Church and State. Megan speaking."

"Megan. This is Liam. How are you?"

"Great, and I've got some excellent news."

"What?" Liam plugs his ear to hear over the end-of-the-week din.

"We received a letter today from Principal Craney."

"Finally. What does it say?"

"No coach at Horizon High School will lead or conduct prayers before, during, or after games or practices. Any violation will be grounds for disciplinary action, and this information has been conveyed to all coaches at Horizon High School."

"That's exactly what we asked for."

"Yes," Megan says. "Principals usually respond this way when they're reminded of the law."

"Awesome." Liam pounds his locker so hard, kids turn to stare. Coach Kloss is going to have to change. "We did it."

"You did it," Megan says. "You're the one who initiated it."

Liam picks up his pack, but then remembers his conversation with Drake. "Megan, the captain of the team says he's leading prayers after games now. He says they're voluntary. That's not much of a change."

"Sure it is," Megan says. "Coaches leading prayers is unconstitutional, and our Constitution is only as strong as the people willing to stand up for it. You did that, and it has an impact now and for all the students who follow you. You got people at your school talking about this. You've accomplished more than you realize."

Liam throws his pack over his shoulder. Maybe she's right. Coach Kloss can't pressure players that way anymore. He rubs the stone in his pocket. Calling Megan also got him to Jack and the girls' team. It got him to Darius and the guys at the B-CAB. It's impossible to imagine not playing with all of them. "Megan, thanks for everything."

"Thank you, Liam. Thanks for having the courage to stand up."

Liam flips his phone shut and closes his locker.

The tape is starting to curl. He smooths it back in place. "Yep." He pumps his fist. "I do."

XXX Liam races home and tells Mom the news in a rush of words.

"That's wonderful." She wraps him in a bear hug. "Congratulations."

"I still can't believe it." Liam untangles himself. "Principal Craney agreed to everything."

"He had to," Mom says. "The law is clear, and principals have to follow the law."

"I wonder what Coach Kloss will do?" Liam grabs a Dr Pepper from the fridge and pops it open.

"He'll follow the law. Or quit coaching. I thought Craney should have fired him for lying to you when you went to him with your concerns."

Liam relaxes on the couch. That's Mom. She always wants more. But her instincts about Coach Kloss not changing without pressure were right. Even though he hates to admit it, her instincts are often right. He doesn't need to tell her that, though.

"A lot of people want Kloss fired. Not making the play-offs is worse to them than leading prayers in the locker room." She sits down in the green chair. "So, now that you've accomplished this, what's next?"

"I'm going to take it easy." Liam leans back.

"Have you been studying your vocabulary for the PSAT?"

"What?" Is she kidding?

"Vocabulary. Have you been studying for the PSAT?"

Liam looks at her like she's from Mars. How can she go from Principal Craney's letter to the PSAT like that?

"Liam, I asked you a question."

"I know. I'm not going to answer." He stares at the painting above the fireplace that Mom made in art school. He sees shadows he's never noticed.

"What do you mean?"

"That's good. You should go back to painting."

"What are you talking about? We're talking about you."

"Let's talk about you for a change." Liam sits up. "Do you miss painting?"

"Liam, I asked you about the PSAT."

"I've got plenty of time." He drains the can in one long gulp.

"You have to think about it. The PSAT is your future. Your scores determine your college choices."

"I'll prepare for it my own way." He looks directly at her.

"What do you mean?"

"I've got my own road, Mom." He smiles. "I must travel it myself."

The Thread

XXX "Who has a poem?" Jack gathers the team around him before the sectional final against Clearwater.

"I do," Iris volunteers. "It's called 'The Way It Is' by William Stafford." She recites from memory:

> There's a thread you follow. It goes among
> things that change. But it doesn't change.
> People wonder about what you are pursuing.
> You have to explain about the thread.
> But it is hard for others to see.
> While you hold it you can't get lost.
> Tragedies happen; people get hurt
> or die; and you suffer and get old.
> Nothing you do can stop time's unfolding.
> You don't ever let go of the thread.

"Thank you, Iris." Jack looks around at the team. "There is a thread you follow, and you have all followed it here.

You've followed it for years — through all the hours of practice, through all the games. Tonight, have fun. Be present. Don't let go of the thread."

Liam and Darius sit in the first row behind the bench. Last night, Horizon won by eleven to put them here. One more win to go to State.

The gym is packed. All kinds of kids who've never been to a girls' hoops game are here because a trip to State means two days off from school and blowout parties. "Let's go, Blazers. Destroy them," hollers a linebacker who's started partying early.

"Go Red! Go White! Go Blazers. All right!" The cheerleaders dance around in front of the Horizon student section.

Liam studies Clearwater. They've got size and a quick left-handed point guard. They've won three games in the playoffs by big margins, just like Horizon. At this point, the remaining teams are all good. "What do you think?" He turns to Darius.

"Simmons is tough." Darius watches the guard making three-pointers. "And Cartwright's strong underneath. Leah and Jess are going to have their hands full."

Jessica goes up against Cartwright, who's got three inches on her. Cartwright wins the tip and Horizon sets up on defense. The person Iris guards has a height advantage of a couple of inches, too. Simmons feeds the ball to Cartwright and the referee blows her whistle. "Foul on forty-four, Red."

Jessica, who barely touched her, turns away in disbelief.

"Let them play, ref." Liam recognizes Mom's voice. She's standing and shouting while Dad tugs at her arm. Liam didn't know they were coming.

Simmons zips past Leah for a layup. She's the best opponent Leah's faced all year.

On offense, Leah goes right at Simmons and draws a foul. Liam claps. Leah's fearless. She sinks both free throws to tie it up, and the Horizon crowd stomps their feet and cheers.

Back and forth they go. Neither team is able to go up by more than four. Clearwater's outside shooters drain any open shot, so Leah and Chloe have to stay with them when the ball goes inside. That leaves Jessica and Iris battling underneath with taller opponents. Iris calls out a back screen for Jessica and jumps out on the switch.

"Watch forty-one," Darius calls. Forty-one bumps Jessica as she sets the screen. Jessica pushes past her and the whistle blows.

"Foul on forty-four, Red." The ref singles out Jessica. "White ball."

"Time-out." Jack signals.

Leah makes a T with her hands and the ref calls time.

"They're calling it close underneath," Jack says. "Jess, you've already got two. Avoid silly fouls. Leah, speed up the pace a bit."

Liam's right heel taps a fast beat. Playing provides a way to burn off some of the energy. Sitting here watching is harder. Darius stands up and sits down twice during the time-out. He's feeling it, too.

XXX Right before halftime, Iris is fouled on a move to the hoop. "Two shots," the ref calls.

Iris stands over to the side at her new free throw spot.

The ref waits under the basket, expecting her to move to the middle. Iris points to her spot and the ref passes her the ball.

She spins the ball, lines up the seams, and shoots. The first shot is good. She shoots again and makes it. Horizon's down by one. Cartwright passes the ball in and Simmons launches up a desperation shot at the buzzer. It falls short.

Liam and Darius go down to the concession stand at halftime. "Two fouls on Jessica." Liam squirts mustard on his hot dog. "She's got to adjust to the refs."

"Yeah," Darius says. "We can't afford to have her sit."

"What do you think Jack's talking about in the locker room?"

"Who knows?" Darius laughs. "Maybe some sixteenth-century Chinese potter."

"Or Arapaho warriors on a buffalo hunt."

"He might not be talking at all."

"Maybe they're doing lights-out visualization," Liam says. "With him, you never know."

In the second half, Jessica picks up her third foul on a drive to the basket. Close call. It could have gone either way.

Iris switches over to guard Cartwright even though she gives up a lot of height. She races downcourt to set up and keep Cartwright from posting up under the basket.

Iris grabs a rebound and passes to Leah. Leah jets up the floor and finds Chloe on the wing. Chloe goes strong to the basket, and Cartwright bumps her. Liam watches the ball roll around the rim twice and then fall in.

Darius nudges Liam. "Look." He points to Chloe, who's on the floor, grabbing her ankle and grimacing in pain.

"Where's the foul on that?" Jack yells.

Leah calls time-out and the trainer runs out to examine Chloe.

"Call the foul when our player gets hit in midair." Jack's going at it with the ref. "You can't call it tight underneath and then let that go."

"That's enough." The ref raises her hand for calm and walks away.

Jack follows her. "You need to protect the players on both teams."

The ref blows her whistle and dramatically signals a T at Jack. "Technical foul, Red. One shot."

Leah rushes in, grabs Jack, and turns him toward the bench. "Calm down, Jack. We need you."

Jack glares at the ref. His face is red with anger. Liam's surprised to see this side of him. Maybe that's why Jack's always telling them to relax — maybe he knows how easy it is to lose it in the heat of a game.

Iris and Jessica support Chloe as she limps gingerly off the court. She can't put any weight on her left foot. The fans stand and applaud as she wipes her hand across her eyes.

"Nikki." Jack waves her over. "Go in for Chloe. Take a deep breath. Relax." He sounds like he's reminding himself as much as her. "Box out. Go after every rebound, every loose ball. Make the extra pass. You know what to do."

Leah passes to Jessica, who turns baseline, stops, and spins the other way. Simmons is waiting for her and falls to the floor.

The ref blows her whistle. "Foul on forty-four, Red."

"That's a flop," Jack says. "She was falling down before she got touched."

"Bad call." Liam stomps his foot.

"Smart play by Simmons," Darius says. "Four fouls on Jess. They'll go inside every possession."

Simmons passes inside to Cartwright, but Nikki doubles down at the right moment to help out. Iris plays great position defense and denies the entry pass. Jessica moves her feet and avoids fouling. Leah burns up the court to increase the tempo. Both teams are making their shots, and the game moves back and forth with speed and skill.

With twelve seconds left, the game is tied. Leah bounces the ball at the top of the key, fakes a three, and slips past Simmons on a drive to the hoop. Cartwright leaps to alter the shot. The ball rolls around the rim and off. Iris grabs it and goes straight back up. Simmons whacks her on the wrist, and the whistle blows.

"Two shots." The ref holds out her fingers.

Iris looks at the scoreboard and exhales a deep breath. Six seconds left. All she needs to do is make one. She lines up at her spot and the ref passes the ball.

Liam crosses his fingers and buries his head in his hands. He can't look. He can't stand the pressure. It's taking forever.

He peeks up as the Horizon fans explode with cheers. She made it. He jumps up and pounds fists with Darius. Iris made it. Horizon is up by one. Iris smiles and Jessica pumps her fist.

"You're my hero, Iris." Chloe hops up and down on one foot.

Iris bounces the ball at her new favorite spot. She buries the second one. Horizon's up by two.

Clearwater doesn't call time-out to set up a last shot. Instead, Simmons flies down the side.

"No fouls," Jack hollers.

Leah's tight on Simmons.

"No fouls!"

"Four, three," Horizon fans count down the clock.

Cartwright sets a screen and Leah slams into it.

"Two, one."

Simmons launches the ball from half-court.

"Zerooooooooooooooo."

Everybody watches the ball in the air.

No way.

No way.

It's going to be close.

The ball hits the backboard and banks in.

It's good. Three points. Clearwater wins.

The Clearwater players scream and pile on top of Simmons, while the Horizon players stare in disbelief.

Leah has an arm around Iris. Jessica barks at the ref about the fouls. Leah leads the team over for the post-game handshake with Clearwater. She hugs Simmons, the player who kept her from going to State. Chloe hops along on some crutches somebody has found for her.

"Over here," Jack says. The girls put their arms on one another's shoulders as they surround him. "That's a tough loss." He takes off his glasses and wipes a towel across his face. "I know all of you are feeling it deeply." He drops the towel to the floor. "You were right there. You battled and gave everything you had. Tonight's a game you'll remember the rest of your lives." Jack looks around. "I'm proud of you."

Liam wipes his eyes and bows his head. It's over. The season is finished.

"One more thing," Jack says. "Don't ever let go of the thread."

XXX "What about these roses?" Mom and Dad are sitting together in front of a crackling fire, looking through a seed catalog when Liam gets back.

"That variety won't grow in our zone," Dad says. "Too cold."

"Of course," Mom says. "I forgot to check if they were suitable for Siberia."

"These ones will work." Dad turns back a couple of pages.

"I'm sorry, Liam," Mom says. "I thought we won with those free throws."

"What a game." Dad sets the catalog down. "Horizon played great."

"Yeah." Liam sits down in the chair. He picks up the bowl Jack made for him from its spot on the coffee table. He runs his fingers over its surface. "Dad, do you see now why I'm glad I practiced with the girls' team rather than sticking it out with Coach Kloss?"

"I do."

"Have a chocolate." Mom offers Liam the box. "Your dad picked up an early Saint Patrick's Day present."

Liam chooses a leprechaun. "Dad, we haven't played Around the World in a long time. I've got a new version and I can beat you."

"We'll see," Dad says. "I've been practicing myself."

Mom's looking at her painting. "Tell him what you told me the other day, Liam."

"What?"

"About your road."

"I've got my own road, Dad. I must travel it myself."

Dad smiles. "Whitman. You've been reading Whitman?"

Liam nods. Dizzy pads over and jumps in his lap. Liam strokes her back as she purrs contentedly.

"He's one of my favorites," Dad says. "Mrs. Stabenow is having you read Whitman for English?"

"No." Liam shakes his head. "I'm reading him for basketball."

Challenged

XXX Liam holds his phone out like he's waiting for it to talk to him. The silver lining of losing last night is that Jack's rule number three is over. He takes a deep breath and punches numbers.

"Hey, Iris. It's me, Liam."

"Hi."

"You played so well last night. I still can't believe it. I can't believe the season is finished."

"I know," she says. "It ended too quickly."

"Yeah. I keep seeing that last shot floating toward the hoop. I keep hoping it's going to miss."

"It's not going to, though."

"Iris."

"Yes?"

"Jack told me when I started practicing that one of his rules was no dating anyone on the team during the season. Now that the season's over, I've been thinking. Do you want to go to a movie? Will you go out with me?"

Iris doesn't respond. He's made a huge mistake. It's too soon. He should have waited a few more days. Why did he have to be so impatient?

"I can do the first one," she says quietly. "Not the second."

"What do you mean?"

"I don't date boys."

What? Are her parents that strict? "Why not?"

"I'm not into boys that way."

The silence hangs.

"Liam, are you there?"

"Yeah, I didn't know." He almost says I'm sorry, but that wouldn't sound right. What signs did he miss?

"My good friends know," she says. "And you're a good friend now."

"Thanks." Liam bites his lip.

"We can still go to a movie, though. I like hanging out with you."

"Okay." One out of two is so much less than he was hoping for.

XXX The all-school assembly to honor girls' basketball, boys' wrestling, and mock trial is the last period of the day. Jack invites Liam and Darius to sit with the team. Seth's sitting beside Coach Kloss on the other side of the auditorium. Both Coach and Seth pretend not to see him.

Jack calls out the players' names one by one and they come onto the stage. Leah whispers something in his ear and he laughs. Chloe hops up on her crutches and waves. Jessica gives Jack a bear hug, lifts him off the ground, and whirls him around.

When the entire team is on stage, Jack leans toward the microphone. "We'd like to recognize two other individuals who have been valuable to our team: Darius Buckner and Liam Bergstrom. Please come up."

The audience applauds while Liam and Darius pound fists. As they climb the steps, their teammates break into a cheer. "Vada vim. Vada vom. Yom. Yom. Yom. Go Darius! Go Liam!"

Liam shakes Jack's hand. "Thanks, Jack. The river is never the same twice."

Jack beams. "I'm honored you remembered."

As Liam walks back to his seat, he catches Drake's eye and gives him a thumbs up.

XXX After the assembly, Drake finds Liam in the hall. "What's that supposed to mean?" He imitates the thumbs up.

"It means you're the greatest, Drake."

"You're so full of it and so is Buckner. That whole girls' team thinks they're superior."

"They are. Twenty-four and two. What were you guys again?"

"What?" Drake looks confused.

"Oh, that's right. Eleven and thirteen," Liam says. "I guess we were better."

"Prove it," Drake says. "You and Darius and any three girls against our starting five. We'll play at the Y. No subs. First team to one hundred. We'll see who's better."

"We don't need to prove anything." Liam walks away. "We know what we can do."

✕✕✕ Liam joins the team at lunch, and before he can say anything, Leah holds up her hand. "Drake already challenged us. We've been discussing it."

"There's nothing to discuss," Jessica snaps. "He's a loser on a losing team. We don't need to play losers."

"Of course we don't," says Leah. "But it would be fun to beat them and shut them up. Besides, I hate ending my season with a loss. I'd like one more game."

"Do it. Do it. Do it." Chloe bangs her crutches. "I'd play if I could." She lifts up her ankle. "Beat them for me."

"What do you think, Darius?" Leah asks.

"If you want to hoop, I'm ready."

"Me, too," Liam adds.

"What about you, Iris?" Leah leans over.

"I don't need to play them, but if you want to, I will."

"We need you, Jess," Leah pleads. "Pretty please with sugar on top."

"Okay. Let's kick their butts."

XXX From the start, the game at the Y is physical. Drake elbows Liam on a screen.

"Keep your elbow in, Drake, or I'll break it off." Liam's picked up some talk from the college guys, and Drake looks surprised.

Nielsen hammers Iris on the arm and she calls a foul.

"Strong move, Iris!" Chloe shouts. Liam lines up in the lane. He can't believe how many girls have come to watch: the rest of varsity, girls from JV and the ninth-grade team, and even some girls who don't play hoops. Only one other guy is watching: Seth.

Iris bounces the ball at her new spot.

"You can't shoot there." Gund bends over with his hands on his knees. The guys are struggling for breath because they haven't played for a couple of weeks.

"Of course I can." She buries them both.

"Pelke loves to go middle," Liam tells Iris as they move back on defense. Staley shoots a long jumper and Liam holds his ground in front of Drake on the box out. Drake slides baseline, but Liam pushes back with his butt and jumps for the rebound. He clears it to Leah, and she flies down-court. She whips a pass to Darius at the arc. His three hits all net.

Trailing thirty-four to twenty-eight, Drake bounces the ball off his foot out of bounds.

"It went off you, Drake," Liam calls.

"Off you." Drake gets in Liam's face.

"That's crazy." Liam wipes the sweat from his forehead with his jersey. "Shoot for it."

Drake shoots from the top of the key and misses.

"Justice." Liam grabs the rebound.

Leah zips a pass to Iris, who finds Liam, who's fouled. He lines up at his new spot for free throws. Leah, Jess, and Iris are so good at passing the ball and finding the open person that it's fun to finally play with them, rather than against them.

Drake takes out his mouth guard. "Do you shoot from the same place as your girlfriend?"

"She's my teammate." Liam bounces the ball. "Remember team spirit?" He hits both of them.

Darius rains in threes. Leah's finding him perfectly off Iris's screens, and Staley is too slow to cover him. Gund switches over on him, so Darius posts him up and takes him to school.

Pelke turns middle and Iris blocks the shot. It bounces right off his head. "Great block, Iris," Chloe shouts. "Next time, shove it down his throat."

Darius jets downcourt and drives into the lane. Drake steps up, so Darius bounce-passes to Liam, who catches the ball and banks it in.

"Good finish, Norbert," Darius shouts.

Liam feels the bounce in his step as he boxes out and grabs rebound after rebound. He rebounds from Coach Kloss and quitting the boys' team. He rebounds from Mom's pressure and Dad's disappointment. He rebounds from Mackenzie. That's life. Things go bad. You rebound.

Darius lines up for a free throw late in the game. They're ahead of the boys' team ninety-four to eighty-four. Pelke stands next to Iris and pushes an elbow against her. "How many of you are lesbians?"

"None of your business," Jessica snaps.

Iris steps back, like she's been slapped.

"He's desperate," Leah says. "Desperate, ignorant, and a bigot — the trifecta."

"What do you mean?" Pelke shrugs. "I was just asking."

"Knock it off, Pelke." Liam glares at him.

"Remember, Pelke," Darius says. "I've seen you naked." He holds up his thumb and index finger close together. "There's a little thing I could talk about if you want to go that way."

Jessica bursts out laughing.

"What are you laughing at?" Pelke asks.

"A teensy-tiny thing." She holds her thumb and finger so close together, they're almost touching. Chloe cracks up and the other girls on the sidelines laugh as Pelke retreats downcourt.

Gund forces a three trying to cut the deficit, and Jessica pushes against Nielsen for the rebound. She passes to Leah, and Liam races downcourt on the break. Leah fakes to him and passes behind her back to Iris, who goes in for the score. The girls watching go nuts. Ninety-six to eighty-four.

Jessica and Iris double-team Nielsen and Iris steals the ball. She passes to Darius, who brings it upcourt. He bounces the ball between his legs at the arc. He can blow by Gund anytime he wants. Instead, he passes to Liam, who's guarded closely by Drake.

"Take him," Darius says.

Liam turns and pump-fakes. Drake's too eager for the block and leaves his feet. Liam goes up and under for the hoop.

"That's it." Darius slaps his hand.

Back at the other end, Staley knocks down a three when Leah gets stuck behind Nielsen's screen.

"Ninety-eight to eighty-seven. Game point." Leah bounces the ball and Liam calls for the ball. He's not just a rebounder; he's got game. He wants to go right back at Drake. Leah passes to Darius on the wing and Darius feeds him. Liam turns baseline and spots Iris open at the edge of the free throw line. He bounce-passes to her, and Pelke's slow to close. Iris shoots.

"Game," she calls as the ball leaves her hand. Everyone

stops to watch the shot. Nothing but net, and the girls watching burst into cheers.

Liam hugs Iris, and Leah, Darius, and Jessica wrap their arms around them. Girls swarm in from the side.

"Leah, you got your win." Liam bows his head against hers in the inner circle of teammates.

"So did you." She smiles.

Liam looks over at the guys, who still can't believe they got beat by thirteen.

Staley comes up and slaps his back. "Good run, Bergie."

"Thanks, man."

"Good game," Nielsen says as he hurries past.

Drake is already at the bleachers, taking off his shoes. Liam walks over. "Good game."

"Whatever." Drake tosses his shoes into his Adidas bag.

Pelke grabs his stuff and scrambles to the door without talking to anyone.

Liam goes up to Seth, who's putting on his jacket. "Hey."

"Those girls are good," he says. "You played great."

"Thanks."

"I was sure you'd get blown away. Instead you played like a monster." Seth jams his hands in his pockets. "Maybe we'll get a chance to play like that together on varsity next year."

"We'll see," Liam says. "Maybe with Darius."

Opening

XXX Leah's opening reception at the Regional Art Center is packed with friends, family, and teammates. Mom greets Jack and Mrs. Jack enthusiastically. Dad sets out a new tray of cookies, and Chloe picks out a rosette and talks to him. She's wearing a shiny silver dress that twirls when she turns. Liam's so used to seeing her hair pulled back for games and practice that he does a double take. She looks good with it down.

He spots Iris in the corner, gazing at a painting. He grabs a couple of ginger thins and walks over. "Cookie." He offers her one.

"Thanks." She's wearing a blue sweater that highlights her eyes. "Check this out."

Liam looks at a painting splashed with jagged strokes of red and white around the outside and a circle of gold in the middle. "What's it called?"

Iris bends down to read the tag. "Jack."

Liam stands back. Quiet in the center, but intense with the colors of Horizon basketball. "That works."

Iris gestures at a dark-haired girl pouring punch into glasses. "That's Hannah, Leah's sister. She's in eighth grade and plays point. She might be good enough to start for us next year."

Liam rubs his freshly shaved chin. Iris, Jess, and Chloe will be back next year. Another Braverman to handle the ball. That's already a strong team. What about the boys? Drake, Nielsen, Gund, and Pelke will all be gone, and Kloss might not be the coach. Would Liam start? Would Seth? Would Darius come back if Kloss didn't? He's got to find a way to keep playing with Darius.

Iris grabs his arm. "Look."

Walking in together are Jessica and Hunter Nielsen, and they're both smiling. Maybe she felt sorry after beating him. No, that wouldn't be like Jess. Maybe she likes him.

Mom and Dad approach Liam. "What a turnout," she says. "We've never had so many tall people, so many young people. So many tall, young people."

"Mom, Dad, this is my friend Iris."

"Nice to meet you, Iris." Dad shakes her hand.

"You're the one who hit those free throws against Clearwater." Mom reaches out to her. "That should have won the game. Those refs were terrible. They stole it."

Iris laughs and Liam shakes his head. That's Mom.

"You played a strong game, Iris," Dad says.

"Thanks, Mr. Bergstrom."

"Here are the Buckners." Mom pulls Dad away to talk with Darius's parents.

"Chloe and I are going to a movie after this." Iris offers him an Altoid. "She wants you to come, too."

"She does?" Liam sucks on the mint. "Are you trying to set me up, Iris?"

"Maybe." She grins. "She's a friend. You're a friend. I look out for my friends."

Leah and Chloe walk over as the warm light of spring pours through the front windows.

"This is an amazing opening, Leah." Liam gestures at all the people.

"Thanks." She's a couple of inches taller in her maroon heels.

"It's the equinox today," he says. "The same amount of light as dark."

"I didn't know that." She adjusts her necklace. "That's good timing for an opening. Now I feel slightly better balanced."

More people come up to congratulate her, and Liam turns to Chloe.

"Hey." He holds out his hand and Chloe takes it. She's got long, dark lashes. "Nice dress."

"Thanks." She smiles.

He breathes in her perfume. Sweet and clean. "I talked with Iris."

"And?"

"A movie together sounds fun."

"Good. I think so, too."

"Hey, Norbert, Chloe." Darius comes up. "Am I interrupting?"

"No. Hey, D." Liam lets go of Chloe's hand and pounds fists with Darius.

"I'll see you later." Chloe waves.

"Definitely." Liam moves closer to Darius. "Thanks, man."

"For what?" Darius shakes the ice in his glass.

"For everything. For quitting the boys' team. For saying yes to Jack. For pushing me in practice."

"You made yourself better, Norbert. And I enjoyed destroying those losers with you."

"I've got one question." Liam puts his hand on Darius's shoulder.

"What?"

"You remember Jack's rule on dating team members?" Liam looks over at Leah. "Did you two wait until the season was over?"

Darius's deep laugh rumbles. "Not quite."

Liam laughs, too. "I didn't think so."

Darius picks an ice cube out of the glass and pops it in his mouth. "Hey, we're playing at the B-CAB tomorrow. We need you."

"I'll be there." Liam grins. "Ready to run."

About the Author

XXX John Coy grew up playing football and basketball, and he worked as a tour guide, dishwasher, and mattress maker before turning to writing full-time. He is the author of numerous award-winning picture books, including *Night Driving*, winner of the Marion Vannett Ridgway Memorial Award for outstanding debut picture book and a *New York Times* Best Illustrated Book of the Year; *Strong to the Hoop*, an ALA Notable Book; and, most recently, *Around the World*, an NBA Read to Achieve selection. His first novel, *Crackback*, was published to great acclaim by Scholastic Press in 2005. John is a member of the NBA Reading All-Star Team and a visiting writer at schools across the country. He lives in Minnesota and loves to travel. Visit John Coy at www.johncoy.com.